THE SLAVES OF SUMURU

SAX ROHMER

THE SLAVES OF SUMURU
SAX ROHMER

ISBN: 1-59654-448-1

BLACKMASK IS AN IMPRINT OF
DISRUPTIVE PUBLISHING.

CHAPTER ONE

I

It was a sinister night. Fine drizzle fell. The higher buildings were beheaded by mist. After-theatre traffic had dwindled to nothing. The great metropolis settled down to that uneasy twilight sleep which is the nearest approach to slumber the Manhattan Babylon ever knows.

High up in the mist, in a domed room resembling in proportions a large tent, the note of a silver bell sounded sweetly. The dome, which had no visible windows, was painted sky-blue. It rested on pillars covered in Arab mosaic, and between the pillars its walls were intricately panelled with inlaid designs of ivory and semi-precious stones. The tiled floor was strewn with mink rugs.

There was a round pool in the floor into which a bronze nymph poured a tiny cascade from a jar balanced on one shoulder. It fell amongst the leaves of water-lilies which floated on the pool. Sometimes, large, brilliantly red fish could be seen gliding between the lily-stems.

Banks of mimosa surrounded the pool, giving out an almost overpowering perfume.

A door concealed in one of the panelled walls opened silently and a man came in. His movements were so leisurely as to convey an impression that he walked in his sleep. He wore a black robe, a skull cap and red slippers. His face, seen in the light from four silver mosque lamps hung on chains from the dome, presented a smiling mask of old ivory.

His slippers made a soft shuffling sound on the tiled floor but no sound when they sank into the softness of the mink rugs. He crossed to the dais, which was veiled by pink silk curtains, and went up the steps, drawing the drapes aside. This produced a faint musical tinkling like that of tiny bells. He touched forehead and breast with both hands and stood there, his head bowed in respect.

"Madonna?"

Madonna reclined amongst the cushions on a deep divan which was upholstered in mink of the same rare quality as that of the many rugs spread about the room. She wore the trousered indoor dress of an Eastern woman, of so flimsy a texture that it exposed rather than concealed the contours of a perfect figure. Her hair was entirely hidden by a close-fitting turban. Her eyes, which were superb, were raised to the man's pale face as she spoke, in a voice hauntingly musical but imperious.

"Tell me, Caspar—Ariosto has visited Sister Celeste?"

"He has, my Lady."

Caspar's voice, like his movements, suggested a sleepwalker.

"No one saw him enter?"

"No one, my Lady. Philo and Sanchez covered his entrance. Shortly after he had gone in, a man, suspected to be the new agent known only as The Major, approached the door. He rang the bell. But no one answered. He presently withdrew—"

"Covered?"

"Covered by Sanchez, Madonna."

"Has Sanchez reported?"

"Not yet."

"Does Philo's description help us to identify this man?"

"Philo has not yet returned, my Lady."

My Lady extended white arms, clenched her hands, and then relaxed again.

"I am not at my ease in this strange and barbarous city, Caspar. The beauty of discipline is hard to enforce where everything is so ugly. It was time for a sharp lesson. This will serve to correct others..."

II

A phantom silhouette seen against street lights, Drake Roscoe crossed to the window of Tony McKeigh's darkened room. He peered down.

"I thought so! The man who tailed me is parked in a doorway over there hoping for something to tip him which apartment I'm in. We won't oblige him for the moment. Let's talk in the kitchen. That faces the other way."

"As you say," Tony McKeigh sighed. "Eccentricity in guests should be humoured. Let me get some drinks out before we go."

But in the kitchenette, Drake Roscoe in the only chair and McKeigh seated on the table, they faced one another—and Tony McKeigh knew that Roscoe had some good reason for his mysterious behaviour. He hadn't lost his tropical tan, which made his frank eyes look the brighter, his hair was streaked with grey. But otherwise Drake Roscoe was a young man.

4

It was he who broke the silence, twirling his glass of whisky reflectively.

"Lucky I caught you at home, Mac. We haven't seen much of one another since I got to New York, and I didn't want to drag you into this business—but, now, it looks as though you're dragged."

Tony McKeigh, attached to the New York office of a London newspaper, had been promoted to a captain in World War II and, because of his special training, been posted by the War Office to Intelligence. He had served in the East for a time under Drake Roscoe, who had held a high rank in the American Service.

"Your remarks, though exciting, are obscure. You would make a good announcer, Roscoe; but somebody else would have to write your scripts."

The once-familiar, rather grim smile showed Drake Roscoe's white lower teeth.

"Listen. Ever hear, in London, about a woman known as Sumuru?"

Tony McKeigh paused in the act of filling his pipe.

"No—never. Odd name. Of course, I have been away from London for more than two years."

"She horrified England with a series of crimes ranging from abduction to murder which completely defeated Scotland Yard. I don't believe her name actually appeared in connection with these outrages. The reason seems to be that nobody knows what her real name *is.*"

"You mentioned Sumuru. Japanese damsel?"

"Not a bit of it! No, sir. But I'm told she was married at one time to the Marquis Sumuru—a Japanese diplomat who committed *hara-kiri.* She also seems to have been married to Baron Rikter, the Swedish millionaire, and to Lord Carradale, a wealthy English peer. They're both dead, by the way. Then there was—"

"Pause! Let me take breath—and refill the glasses. This woman is a female Bluebeard!"

"She's something far more dangerous. And unless the Commissioner at Scotland Yard has gone nuthouse, she is now operating in Manhattan!"

Drake Roscoe stood up and began to pace about in an area five feet by four. His conversation resembled irregular fire. Each sentence was a sharp explosion.

"This woman, Mac, is a greater menace than the atom bomb."

Tony McKeigh became conscious of growing excitement. He felt that he stood on the verge of strange things...

"The public doesn't have to suspect. But she, or someone working along identical lines, is established right here, in Manhattan! I handled a similar case some years ago. I've been recalled to deal with this one. It's important my identity shouldn't leak out. So I'm known simply as The Major. Remember that."

He hadn't removed his hat. Under its moist brim, his eyes now looked steely, almost fierce:

"Where had you blown from when you kindly rang my bell just now?"

"I'll tell you. There's a certain Lew Kerrigan, a private eye operating from an office on Broadway. He handles pretty shady cases. We won't call his game blackmail, but—"

"Sounds an interesting squirp." Roscoe's smile was grim.

"I rather imagine he'll come to a sticky end. For your private information, Sally Obershaw—daughter of William Obershaw, the big railroad man—disappeared last week."

"Disappeared? But her pictures were on all the society pages. Most beautiful debutante of the season, and so forth."

"She has vanished! On police advice, it's been kept quiet, so far. But the whole Centre Street outfit has been working day and night on the case. A big reward hangs to it. Roscoe pulled up, stared at Tony McKeigh. "This is the third disappearance of the kind from Manhattan alone quite recently. It's why I'm here!"

"But—"

"All those missing are young girls, and all of them acknowledged beauties."

Tony groped vaguely for a box of matches.

"How on earth have the news-rooms missed this story?"

"Because it's been hushed up. You see, we know Sally's alive."

"Some keen businessman in the slave trade (think of the *nouveaux riches* in the East) is cornering American beauties! What a story!"

Roscoe grasped Tony's shoulder urgently, and his eyes were cold.

6

"I said, Mac, for your private information! If one paragraph breaks, I'll pin it to you."

He held out his hand. Tony grasped it. "Count on me, Roscoe."

"That's fine. You see, I think you may be of use. Listen. Slave traders don't go in for millionaire's daughters! This man Kerrigan got in touch with William Obershaw. He said he had information about the missing Sally. He said he was playing with dynamite, and so—"

"What did Obershaw offer?"

"Obershaw called Headquarters. I was notified and decided to talk to Kerrigan as William Obershaw's representative."

"And where was the conference to take place?"

"Do you know a showy junk shop full of imitation antiques, run by a woman called Celie Artz?"

"Four blocks east of here."

"That's it. And do you know Celie by sight?"

"I have seen her, in passing. She is a glance-worthy brunette, with a statuesque chassis."

And Tony McKeigh was soon to be reminded of those words, so lightly spoke at the moment.

"Well, Kerrigan agreed to meet me there at twelve-thirty tonight, for some reason, but I had planned to arrive ahead of time. And I tried."

"Be more coherent. What do you mean by 'tried'?"

"I mean that *somebody* has the place covered—"

"Police?"

Roscoe shook his head impatiently.

"When I stepped up to the door—it's in a recess—and rang the bell, I could get no reply. But I kept at it. Then I sensed, rather than saw, someone in the shadows only just behind me."

"Where did you hit him?"

"I didn't try it! You see, I have a dossier from Scotland Yard which would scare the lights out of a bulldog. This woman Sumuru employs some of the most ghastly weapons ever invented. She's an adept in the use of obscure poisons. Some of her victims have been blinded by a mere puff of powder; others struck dumb. And there's a horrible thing called *rigor Kubus,* a sort of fungus which invades the system and apparently turns the body to something like stone."

Tony McKeigh finished his second whisky at a gulp.

"I don't think I'm going to like Sumuru."

"You won't! I have an official photograph of a man who died of *rigor Kubus*. It was injected into his neck. I should hate to look like that in a funeral parlour. Where's your phone?"

"Right beside the door in there."

Drake Roscoe went into the dark room and dialled a number, using his flash lamp. There was an interval, and then:

"Busy signal. Suspicious. Something wrong with Celia Artz' line!" came crisply. "This forces my hand."

"What's to do?"

"No choice. I'm sending for a police car. We must force the door. I have an uneasy feeling that Sumuru is a move ahead!"

III

A large plaster cast of Queen Nefertiti dominated the windows of Celie Artz's curio store. Cases of scarabs and Ancient Egyptian jewellery glittered attractively in a subdued illumination. The establishment had closed at seven o'clock, but certain lights remained on all night.

There were mandarin robes half hidden in shadow, to suggest lurking Orientals; ivory statuettes and lacquer and silver boxes; amber and jade. Celie Artz's emporium was an Aladdin's cave, synthetic from wall to wall.

A patrolman materialized out of clammy vapour, tested the fasteners of the door, and peered in at the window. He could just see the handrail of a short stair, where shadows gathered darkly. He shook his head and passed on. Officer Murphy had his own ideas about Celie Artz; but it was none of his business.

The time was just twenty-one minutes after midnight.

Weather and the hour had emptied the streets, so that no one was in sight when an ornamental Chrysler, enamelled Fire Department red, glided to a halt before the shop. A man got out, and the car moved silently away.

This man wore a belted white rainproof over dress-clothes, and his dusky features were shaded by the brim of a soft black hat.

He went into the recess and rang a bell beside the door.

In reply, a figure appeared on the shadowy stair. A woman made her way through the art treasures to admit the visitor. The window lights revealed her as a study in voluptuous curves sheathed in a black frock with a generous neckline. A cigarette dangled from her full lips. She opened the door.

8

"Go right ahead, Lew."

Lew went right ahead. The woman stayed to refasten the door. The place had an aromatic smell, in which sandalwood predominated. At the top of the dim stair was an office, and here the man shed hat and rainproof and adjusted his black bow.

Lew Kerrigan was a dressy figure, short, stocky, almost Moorish of complexion, with a pencil-line moustache and gleaming, wavy, dark hair.

When the woman rejoined him, he threw a muscular arm around her.

"Frightened?"

She drew away.

"No. I'm not frightened. But—"

"But what? You look kind of shaky."

"There was a phone call just before you came, but when I answered, the line had gone dead."

"What about it?"

Kerrigan's keen gaze swept the room. A bottle of whisky stood on a bureau. He saw two empty glasses. He looked up, with narrowed eyes.

"Who's been sampling my thirty years old Bourbon, Celie?"

"Listen, Lew." Celie dropped down on a long stool, facing him. "Even now—I don't think I can go through with it."

Lew Kerrigan crossed to a swivel chair set before a desk. Celie sat watching him bite off the tip of a cigar with teeth keen as a terrier's. He didn't look at her. As he lighted up, he spoke.

"Who's been sampling my nine teen-twenty Bourbon?"

"*She* sent someone to see me."

Lew Kerrigan laid his newly-lighted cigar in a tray. Now, turning, he looked at Celie. Her glance met his own, and her dark eyes were haunted.

"You haven't tried to double on me, Celie?"

His tone was dangerous, but she shook her head unhappily.

"Why ask me that? When this man rang, I opened the door because I thought it was you. When I saw him, I knew that he came from *her*—Our Lady."

Lew Kerrigan banged his fist on the desk.

"Don't talk about her that way! You give me the jitters! She isn't a witch on a broomstick. She's just a female gangster with one hell of a set-up. What Al Capone left behind she plans to pick up. Talk sense. What did this bird say? Is he on to something?"

Celie shook her head again.

"He came to see me about Sally Obershaw—"

"There's nothing on you there! There's no evidence."

"Maybe not. But Ariosto went back over every visit she made. He knew I had orders from Madonna to teach her. I lent her *Tears of Our Lady.* It's the first text-book. Then, when the time came, Madonna met her here, and was satisfied that she was suitable."

"Who's this Ariosto?" Kerrigan growled.

"Our Lady's chief aide. He's a physician."

"Her boy friend, huh?"

"No. You'll never understand—but he isn't. He's a very clever man, and he scared me to-night. He said there was a nation-wide search for Sally, that a big reward hung on it—"

"You mean he hinted you might be tempted to squeal?" Celie shook her head in a way which suggested resigned despair.

"Not just that. But he did seem to suspect a leakage. The Bourbon was my idea. I felt I needed it."

"Did he mention my name?"

"No. But it nearly drove me crazy to think what would happen if you or the other one arrived while he was here. Someone kept ringing the street bell. But Ariosto wouldn't let me answer it. He hasn't been gone five minutes. I said I had a headache and must go to bed."

Lew Kerrigan stood up, stuck the still smouldering cigar between his teeth, and took two clean glasses from the bureau. He walked into an adjoining room and came back with a pitcher of ice-water. Then he mixed two big drinks and handed one to Celie, who hadn't stirred. She was very pale.

"Now tell me what you mean by you can't go through with it! I figure on a hundred thousand for what we're going to sell Obershaw. You're scared stiff of this woman, and so we'll leave for Mexico just as soon as I touch the cash."

Celie took the glass, but grasped it clumsily as though her fingers were stiff. She looked up at Lew Kerrigan in a vague way.

"You'll never touch the... cash..."

"What are you talking about?"

"Sally is to be offered up—for acceptance—to-morrow..."

10

"Offered up for acceptance? What's that? Did *you* go through it? Was that when you got that mark put on your ankle?"

Celie nodded, weakly.

"Once any woman... belongs to Our Lady ... no one... can ever get her... away again ..."

Lew Kerrigan stooped and grasped Celie's shoulders roughly.

"Listen. I don't know how much whisky you've had. But if you're not drunk, you're crazy. *I'm* going to get somebody away from her. *It's you!*" He glanced at a gold wrist-watch. "In three minutes our man's due—and we're going to sell him all the information you've passed over to me since the night I first saw that thing tattooed on your ankle..."

IV

The note, of a silver bell still haunted the domed and (perfumed room when Caspar crossed the floor, his slippers whispering on the tiles and ceasing to whisper on the mink. When he opened the rosy curtain which gave out fairy music, the woman reclining on the divan lay there with half-closed eyes, seemingly dozing. But, through heavy lashes, points of light glittered as if from hidden jewels.

"Madonna?"

"Have Philo and Sanchez returned?"

"No, My Lady. Philo is covering the Celie Artz store, and Sanchez has just reported."

"What did he report?"

"That he has not yet identified the apartment to which the man suspected to be The Major went. Sanchez is remaining on watch."

"Sanchez is a fool. And Philo?"

"Philo has reported that Ariosto has rejoined him. I was instructed to silence the Celie Artz line from here, and I have done so."

"Good."

"May I venture to make a suggestion, Madonna?"

"Let it be intelligent."

"I have, naturally, made inquiries about The Major. What has occurred to-night suggests a possible clue to his identity. A man called McKeigh lives on the street to which the suspect went from Celie Artz. McKeigh is employed by a London newspaper—"

11

"How do you know all this?"

"Madonna, I live to serve you. I make it my business to learn all I can about a handsome man—when I chance to see one—or a beautiful girl."

Madonna's long lashes flickered, but were not raised.

"Your slave-trading instincts are invaluable to me, Caspar. But what has the personable young man McKeigh to do with The Major?"

"He is a friend, My Lady, of a certain Drake Roscoe, whose recent appearance greatly alarmed me. Roscoe is a special agent sometimes employed by Washington. Roscoe and The Major may be the same..."

There were some moments of silence, interrupted only by the plashing of the fountain. One might have wondered where this strange room was located. It was so still. No whisper of a busy city penetrated to it.

"Where is Ariosto?"

"He is with Philo, Madonna."

"Why does he not report to me? How am I to know if he has succeeded? It is impossible for me to act until I know this."

The golden voice was vital. The beautiful body remained inert, and then:

"Who is on duty to-night, Caspar?" My Lady asked softly.

"Sister Viola, Madonna."

"Send her to me. Leave the curtains open."

Caspar saluted profoundly and retired. As he went out by the door hidden in the panelled wall, his voice sounded dimly:

"Sister Viola is wanted by Our Lady."

As the door closed, other voices, further away, and very dim, echoed the call:

"Sister Viola is wanted—"

"Sister Viola..."

A second door opened, a door as silent as the first, and a girl came in. She was a very pretty girl, a mass of chestnut hair framing her charmingly piquant face. Her composure was admirable, but evidently kept up with difficulty.

She crossed to the dais and stood there with lowered head, her hands folded before her.

"You sent for me, Madonna."

"Yes, child. Sit there and listen to me."

The girl, who wore a plain dinner-frock, dutifully took a seat upon a cushioned Egyptian stool near the divan. Madonna fixed her wonderful eyes upon her and smiled.

"You are my latest disciple, Viola. Soon you will be called upon to receive another sister, if she meets with our approval as you did."

And Sister Viola became lost in the deep well of those great eyes, swept away by the harp-notes in that exquisite voice.

"You know our creed, Viola—to restore beauty to a world grown ugly. And to bring about its success, we must sometimes use ugly methods. You are trembling, Viola."

"No, dear My Lady! I was listening intently."

"I never use what is ugly except to aid what is beautiful. Our order already is very rich, although not yet as rich as the Church of Rome. Unfortunately, the Roman Church regards us unfavourably. You were educated in a French convent—" Sister Viola lowered her eyes. "You speak French as freely as you speak English. You are highly intelligent. You have beauty. We have a dangerous enemy, Viola. He is known simply as The Major. I believe I have discovered his identity. To-night it will be your duty to prove, or to disprove, my theory..."

CHAPTER TWO

I

An uneasy silence had fallen in Celie Artz's office. Lew Kerrigan helped himself to another drink. Celie didn't seem to hear when he asked her to join him. He had been priming himself pretty freely for the coming interview with William Obershaw's representative. (He took it for granted this would be an attorney, and Lew knew he skated on thin ice.) But he couldn't account for his feelings. Anger with Celie predominated. So he took another drink.

At last a chance had come to clean up in a big way. Sally Obershaw was in the hands of some sort of secret society to which Celie also belonged. He knew most, if not all, that Celie knew about it. He knew where they met. He knew where Sally was to be found. He didn't know the identity of the extraordinary woman who controlled this thing. He made a note in a small memo-book and put the book in his pocket again.

He dropped back in the swivel-chair and looked at his wrist-watch. The hand seemed to be dancing about. Was he getting drunk?

"This guy's late," he growled.

The time was thirty-five minutes after midnight.

Celie stood up, slowly, unsteadily. She moved stiffly towards her bedroom.

"What's going on? Our man's due any minute!"

"Must ... lie down..."

She staggered through the doorway. Lew Kerrigan stood up and stared after her. Was she really ill? Or was she pretending to pass out so that her evidence wouldn't be available when William Obershaw's representative arrived?

He clenched his fists, stayed silent, and sat down again. He'd have her out when she was wanted.

But he became more and more aware of most curious sensations. In the first place, he was disinclined to make any effort, mental or physical. A sort of lassitude stole over him.

Who was this woman that Celie called "Our Lady"? It wasn't possible that Celie didn't know, although she had sworn to him that no one knew. He felt very drowsy. Where, for hell's sake, was the man from Obershaw? Then, his left hand developed cramp, and he moved it from the arm of the chair and opened and closed his fingers to restore circulation.

What was really wrong with Celie? Could there be such a thing as a witch, in Manhattan, to-day?

All sorts of voices sounded in his ears. They screeched: "Yes!"

They seemed to be the voices of inanimate things. An ivory statuette was laughing at him! The half-empty whisky bottle said "Yes"—in a deep bass voice!

He had overdone it. This was the beginning of *delirium tremens*!

Lew Kerrigan heaved himself to his feet. His limbs felt like bars of lead. His heart seemed to be bursting. There was a haze in the room—a purple haze.

"Celie!"

His voice was a husky whisper—or sounded like that to himself.

He staggered to the open doorway, moving like an automaton that was running down. But he made it, clutched the frame with fingers which registered no contact, and stared into the lighted bedroom.

Only for a moment he stayed there. Then, uttering an inhuman cry, a stifled scream like that of some wordless animal, he turned and stumbled blindly out.

He fell down the stairs into the antique store. But Lew Kerrigan heard nothing of the glass and china crashes which resulted from his fall.

It was—it must have been—a superhuman effort which enabled him to stand upright again. For he got to the door, opened it, and ran out on to the street—screaming, wordlessly screaming.

And, always the screams grew less—and less—and less...

II

Tony McKeigh took up his hat and coat, and then threw them down again. His emotions defied analysis. The wail of the police car which recently had taken Roscoe away had stirred memories of air raids he had known, and had left him with an uncanny sense of impending danger. He had watched the departing car from the window.

What was happening—maybe had happened already—at that strange rendezvous in Celie Artz's junk shop? Who was this shadowy being, Sumuru, and what were her motives?

He had just begun to fill his pipe when the phone buzzed. He crossed.

"Hullo? Yes—McKeigh here."

"Hold the line." An interval, and then came Drake Roscoe's snappy voice: "You there, Mac? Listen. You have your press card?... Right. Gome along—now. Ask for The Major."

McKeigh was out in the humid night in a matter of seconds. Rain had ceased, but the mist prevailed. He never recalled having seen the streets so deserted. He set out at a brisk pace, for he had only four blocks to go. He went at such a speed, a thousand conjectures outrunning his legs, that he quite failed to sense the presence of a follower.

This follower was a girl, slender and shapely and having a grace of movement which might have belonged to a ballerina. She wore a hooded waterproof cape, but, as she speeded along, the hood had fallen back to reveal hair which gleamed in ever-changing waves of mahogany and chestnut which shimmered and danced when light caressed it.

The strange pursuit continued until, in sight of Cclic Artz's shop, a patrolman stepped out on McKeigh. Another was standing in the middle of the street to divert traffic.

"Street closed. Police operations."

McKeigh had his Press card ready.

"Okay. Go ahead."

He was about to start when a timid touch on his arm pulled him up. He turned and looked down into an oval face which seemed overburdened by the beauty of eyes blue as the Caribbean on a summer's morning.

"I follow you, but you go so fast. Someone who comes out from your door, and goes in a police car, drop this. Can you tell me, please?"

The words were a breathless whisper, the voice and accent he thought adorable. This distracting little beauty was offering him a black leather wallet. He took it without removing his regard from those entrancing eyes.

"May I look?"

"But *certainement.* I mean, surely."

17

McKeigh opened the wallet. It contained nothing but a sealed envelope addressed: "Mr. Drake Roscoe."

He resumed his study of the blue eyes. "I will return it to my friend. Thanks a lot. My name is Tony McKeigh. I'm sure Roscoe would like to thank you, too. I live in Apartment 6b."

Those wonderful eyes were opened widely as the girl stared up at him.

"You are nice," she said. "I am so sorry. Good night."

And with never another word she turned and hurried away!

"She's so sorry!" Tony McKeigh muttered. He watched the fleeting figure until it became lost to view. He still seemed to see those blue eyes. "She's so sorry. Oh, hell!"

The officer was considering him with a stony regard. McKeigh nodded and went on.

Two police cars stood outside Celie Artz's premises, which were fully illuminated. At the barrier at the farther end of the block not more than four or five people had lingered out of curiosity. Two policemen stood in the open doorway.

"McKeigh. The Major expects me."

"Go ahead."

He walked on through the Celie Artz collection, picking his way amongst items which seemed to have been recently broken. Drake Roscoe came out at the top of the stair to meet him.

"Prompt action, Mac. What have you got there?"

"Something you dropped outside my door."

Roscoe turned the wallet over in his hands. "Not mine. Where did you find it?"

McKeigh told him, briefly. "Open it!" he concluded.

Roscoe did so. The wallet contained nothing but an envelope. He stared, and then ripped the envelope. His expression grew grim. "Look!"

The envelope was empty!

"Was she a beauty, Mac?" Drake Roscoe asked. "Sumuru, I'm told, always knows how to pick 'em! I'm spotted already. Oh don't make heavy weather of it! You're new to this game. Wait until I show you what we found inside!"

He led the way through Celie Artz's office to the door of the room beyond. A police captain and two detectives were on duty in there. They saw the horror sweep over McKeigh's face, but said nothing.

"This is how we found her." Roscoe spoke in a hushed voice. "We're waiting for the Medical Examiner."

"But," Tony whispered, "how does she stay upright?"

Celie Artz stood at the foot of an ornately carved antique bed, her left hand clutching one of the two mahogany posts. Her right hand was pressed to her breast. A look of indescribable horror rested on her face, which still retained traces of a once great beauty. A sheath-like black gown defined the lines of that statuesque form and Tony remembered, shuddering, his own words so recently spoken.

"Touch her!" one of the detectives invited grimly, "if you can trust your nerve."

Tony McKeigh glanced from face to face. Everyone watched him, as he stepped forward and laid an unsteady finger on Celie's shoulder. Everyone saw him change colour, saw him conquer revulsion and grasp more tightly.

He was deathly white when he drew back.

"My God! what is it? She's been turned into stone!"

"Evidently, like Lot's wife, she looked back! It's the thing called *rigor Kubus*. I have a detailed account in the dossier from Scotland Yard—"

"We'll have to saw off that bedpost," the police captain said hoarsely, "to get her away. Her fingers are as hard as concrete."

"Where is... Lew Kerrigan?"

Tony didn't know his own voice.

"That's the puzzle," Roscoe snapped irritably. "There are two glasses out there and a nearly empty bottle of whisky. They'll go to the laboratory. There's the butt of a cigar, and a man's rainproof, hat and gloves. But there's no Lew Kerrigan..."

III

In the room with the blue dome, the woman addressed as Madonna had piled cushions on the tiled floor beside the marble pool. She lay prone, one white hand dipped in the water, tempting the big red fish with fragments of food, and laughing like a child when they nibbled it from her fingers.

Her laughter sounded like golden bells.

A man stood watching her. He wore evening dress, and his clothes fitted faultlessly his tall, athletic figure. His face, which would have been handsome if less saturnine, expressed very mixed emotions. There was a rapacious look in his dark eyes as he studied the barely concealed beauty of My Lady's perfect body.

She looked up, still laughing gaily, then twisted around so that she rested on one elbow.

"Ariosto"—the musical voice was low pitched— "why do you persist in desiring me, when you know that I am unattainable?"

He turned his head aside.

"You have been attainable by some—"

My Lady laughed again, softly, now.

"Those I could not chain in my will I chained in my arms. Is that what you mean? I gave you Dolores. She is lovely. Are you tired of her?"

Ariosto didn't reply.

"In you, among all men, this folly is inexcusable." She extended herself languidly, resting her head on the cushions. "I have Caspar's report, but I await details. Tell me—it is finished?"

Ariosto inhaled deeply, and then spoke.

"It is finished. The microscopic spores, as I prepare them, act slowly when swallowed. Inhalation is swift, so is injection. I estimated that the quantity which I placed in Sister Celie's glass—allowing for the counteraction of the whisky—would invade the tissues in thirty minutes. This occurred. I put twice the quantity into the whisky remaining in the bottle, and the man, Kerrigan, succumbed in less than that time. I was waiting with Philo to take care of him. We drove to an agreed spot and disposed of the body."

"They will analyse the contents of the bottle and glasses."

"Undoubtedly. But except for Van Voorden's pamphlets there is no description of this fungus available. It cannot be distinguished from penicillin. Probably I, alone, know how to identify it as I, alone, know how to cultivate it." My Lady looked up suddenly.

"Of course you stripped this man's body?"

Ariosto started, looked away.

"I thought it unnecessary, as it would sink to the bed of the river."

My Lady began to coil her lithe limbs under her in the manner of a puma preparing to spring.

"My friend," she said softly, "my great friend, you are some times a great fool—"

IV

It was very late that night when Drake Roscoe lighted a cigar and lay back in his chair, smoking reflectively. From his open window, had he cared to look out, he could have seen the distant Statue of Liberty floodlighted by its ninety-odd 1,000-watt lamps.

He could also have seen a number of tall buildings, amongst them one towering high above its immediate neighbours, surmounted by an ornamental cupola. But he might have paid no special attention to it.

"In spite of all my precautions, Mac," he said snappily, "this woman had evidently got hold of a clue to my identity. Her method of checking the information was smart, and effective."

"Yes." Tony McKeigh sighed. "I fell for it like a withered leaf."

"Anyone would fall for it."

Roscoe turned to a stack of documents on a table beside him as Tony tapped out his pipe in an ashtray.

"Any bright hints in the Scotland Yard reports?" Tony asked.

"Well"—Roscoe turned over some pages— "there's a fairly complete account, some of it toughly scientific, of the horror called *rigor Kubus.*"

Tony suppressed a shudder and took another drink.

"Don't remind me. Ghastly."

"I'm told"—Roscoe tapped the papers— "that there's an antidote, of sorts, invented by the Dutch scientist, Van Voorden. It has to be used promptly, though."

"They have the remains of the whisky. Analysis should help."

Roscoe shook his head.

"Van Voorden says no. There are no present means of identifying this fungus—except, of course, by giving a dose to somebody!"

"Brr!"

"The reason we decided to release the story is this: Scotland Yard suppressed the facts concerning the first case in England. But someone signing himself M.D. wrote a letter to the *Times* exposing the real symptoms. This M.D. was never traced, by the way. He was, of course, acting for Sumuru."

Tony McKeigh stared. "But with what object?"

21

"Wide publicity! She wants all her crowd to know what happens to anybody crossing her path. You see, this damned woman is apparently the only person who has ever succeeded in cultivating the fungus."

"She must be a fascinating little soul to meet. What does she look like? The Witch of Endor?"

"On the contrary. She's a raving beauty. Several men, including a celebrated French poet, have committed suicide over her!"

"But she can't be any spring chicken, Roscoe."

Roscoe shook his head in bewilderment.

"I agree. She was, reputedly, the Marquise Sumuru early in the war. What she had been before that I don't know."

"What type is this Circe? Ravishing blonde or blinding brunette? Or does she change from time to time?"

"She changes so much from time to time that no two descriptions of My Lady tally in any way!"

"The woman's a chameleon!"

"She is believed to have thousands of followers. And all her women are beauties. Have to be. What about your little friend who handed you the wallet?"

Tony began to refill his pipe.

"She was lovely. Listen, Roscoe, old scout, I don't believe that girl capable of taking part in those gruesome crimes. I just don't believe it."

"H'm." Drake Roscoe carefully dropped a cone of ash from his cigar. "Let me offer a word of advice. Forget her. She belongs to Sumuru, and so she's not fit to belong to anybody else. Probably, Sumuru has one of her agents right here in the hotel, now!"

Tony went on filling his pipe. "Poor Celie Artz was a good-looker. I suppose she was one of the gang?"

"Undoubtedly. And the missing Lew Kerrigan had induced her to squeal. It seems to have been known that the antique shop was a facade for some other business. But the police, having satisfied themselves it wasn't dope, didn't bother any more. I suspect it was a rendezvous for likely disciples."

"But what on earth do they get out of it? What has this woman to offer?"

Drake Roscoe smiled grimly.

"What do people get out of being Fascists, or Communists? It's simply that certain characters have the strange power to inspire in others—*some* others—a fanatical obedience to their crazy ideas. Sumuru is evidently such a character."

Tony closed his tobacco pouch.

"But my dear Roscoe—pause. No nice girl could fail to be entirely devoid of enthusiasm for the bloodthirsty ideas of this female Nero. For instance—do you seriously believe that Sally Obershaw has joined the Witches' Sabbath?"

"All the evidence points that way, doesn't it?"

"It's quite bizarre to my sturdy commonsense that such a female can carry on these antics in New York City and get away with it. She must be rooted out! She must be destroyed! Have you *no* clue to her identity?"

Drake Roscoe replaced the mass of documents from Scotland Yard in a big briefcase and returned the case to a bureau, which he unlocked. He took out a small leather portfolio and opened it before Tony.

"The only known photograph of the Marquise Sumuru!"

Tony suppressed an exclamation of excitement.

"Enlargement of a press picture," he murmured. "Who took it?"

"A *Daily Express* photographer roaming about Mayfair, London, looking for smart women wearing the new Fall fashions. You see—she had just stepped out of a car in Berkeley Square. Scotland Yard was busy for over six months hunting for such a picture, assisted by someone who knew My Lady by sight—Mark Donovan, of the Alliance Press. Happen to have met him?"

"Mark Donovan! Oh, indubitably! A good-looking lad."

"So I believe. He's married, and back here, now, I understand."

The picture showed an exquisitely chic woman wearing a tailored suit and a waist-length mink cape. The suit was of some light material; shoes, gloves and hat were dark... and to the hat was attached a diaphanous veil through which little could be seen of the face except remarkably fine eyes looking out as through a mist.

"Not so hot," Tony murmured. "Very shapely damsel. Legs above reproach. Shouldn't know her, though, if I met her—unless she wore the same outfit."

"It isn't as bad as that, Mac. If you'll glance at the back, you'll see that Yard experts have worked out her approximate height and other dimensions. This isn't without value. The negative is in the envelope pinned to the mount."

Tony was reading the closely-typed particulars when the phone buzzed. Drake Roscoe took the call.

"Hullo! yes? Major here... What? Where are you speaking from? ... I understand. Hold everything until I arrive. Starting now."

He hung up, and turned. His very pose said: "Action!" His eyes were alight, although his smile was dour.

"A clue at last!—They have found Lew Kerrigan..."

CHAPTER THREE

I

"THIS way, sir."

Drake Roscoe and McKeigh stepped out of the car. East River Drive stretched misty and mysterious behind them. There were moving lights on the distant bank and all that subdued night activity which seems oddly furtive, but belongs to any dockland where ships lie moored in shadow.

They followed the police lieutenant into an old and nearly empty warehouse which smelled of tar. Only one lamp—a powerful one—illuminated the echoing interior. It hung directly over a trestle table on which something lay covered under an oilskin sheet. A sergeant of the Marine Division stood near by, and a tall, shaggy man who wore black-rimmed spectacles had just replaced the sheet.

He looked up as Roscoe and McKeigh came in.

"Hullo, Doctor," Roscoe greeted him, for he had recognized the medical examiner. "Finished?"

"Yes, Mr. Roscoe—sorry! Major—"

"You didn't slip up. I'm spotted. 'The Major' is already known to the enemy as Drake Roscoe!"

"You're quick on the job. I was prepared to wait for you." He pulled the oilskin aside. "Here he is. Diagnosis was easy!"

Tony McKeigh drew a deep breath, and clenched his teeth. Active service had inured him to violent death, but—

The body, in a contorted pose, both fists clenched, was that of a man, short and stocky. His original complexion it was impossible to define, for the reason that his skin had assumed a dirty-white colour. He had black hair and a pencil-line moustache. He wore sodden dress clothes.

His features bore an expression of such frenzied horror that Drake Roscoe said shortly:

"Cover him up!"

As the sheet was replaced:

"Two in one night!" the doctor commented. "The tissues are hard as marble. Were in both cases. In many years' experience I've never met with anything like it. Speaking professionally, I would say it's impossible. But the impossible has happened."

Tony McKeigh swallowed, and spoke. He was grateful to the man who had covered up that ghastly exhibit. In some way, it was even more horrifying than Celie Artz.

"Did anyone here know the victim?" Roscoe asked hoarsely.

"Sure. We all knew Lew Kerrigan. Here's what we found on him."

Police Lieutenant Cody stepped to the other end of the table. There was little enough. A pocket torch, a lighter, a packet of cigarettes oozing river water. Two cigars in similar condition, about a hundred dollars in a folder, and a gold wrist-watch; last, but most important, a saturated memo-book with several entries.

"No other papers?"

"Not a thing."

"How did you come to pick him up?"

"Guy on a tugboat saw him thrown in," someone replied. "Two men hauled the body out of an automobile and dumped it in the river. The boys could never have gotten him on the hooks, the way he is, if he'd gone to the bottom. But he fell on a concrete buttress—happens to be right below where they threw him."

As he spoke, a tugboat's whistle moaned out on East River—the East River, from which Lew Kerrigan had been hauled so recently. A night mist was crawling in from the sea. Drake Roscoe stripped his coat off.

"I'll work over this notebook, here and now. We have to move fast..."

He stopped short. A puzzled look crossed his tanned face, and then:

"Mac!" he snapped. "My hotel apartment is probably safe enough—but I quite forgot, like a fool, to lock up the Scotland Yard data, and the photograph!"

"At your service, sir. If in a spot, call Tony McKeigh. I'll nip back, lock up, and wait for you. Okay?"

"Thanks a lot, Mac." Roscoe turned to Lieutenant Cody.

"Call my hotel. Get the night manager. Instruct him to admit Mr. McKeigh to my apartment..."

II

"Thanks!" McKeigh nodded to the clerk from the reception desk as he unlocked Drake Roscoe's door.

As Tony had passed through those fabulous salons below, he had found himself searching wistfully for a glimpse of gleaming, wavy hair—hair unlike any other—for a pair of deep blue eyes. Agents of the supreme mystery, Sumuru, were almost certainly in the hotel by now, as Roscoe had surmised; and he wanted to meet that girl again. He wanted to know why she worked for the most dangerous criminal Manhattan had ever harboured.

"Don't forget to slam the door when you come out," the clerk reminded him.

McKeigh nodded again and went into the lobby. He had his hand raised to the switch, when he paused, stood stock still, and listened.

He had detected a flash of light—no sooner seen than gone—in the living-room, had heard a faint movement!

Now, all was silent. But beyond any shadow of doubt, there was someone in Drake Roscoe's apartment!

Street sounds were dimly audible even at that height; taxi horns, the roar of trucks and buses, even faint voices, He recalled that the window had been left open.

A horrifying memory of a petrified man lying in a desolate warehouse turned him cold. He realized, suddenly, acutely, the fact that he was involved in warfare with an unknown opponent who stuck at nothing.

Yet his hesitation was only momentary. Taking a deep breath, he went in and switched up the apartment lights. Fists clenched, he stood in the doorway, looking around. There was no sound. But he saw at once that the partly opened window was now opened widely—and he saw something else, something which prompted him to move forward, step by step, for a closer view.

A rope ladder, with light, tubular threads, hung outside.

A burglar! And the burglar had escaped!

So thought McKeigh, and leaning out, was about to look dizzily upwards, when there came a patter of swift footsteps from behind him. He withdrew his head, turned in a flash and saw her.

His wish had been fulfilled.

She had actually reached the lobby when he sprang and held her locked fast in his arms!

"Seems I arrived in time!" he said.

His heart was beating rapidly. A sudden pallor which had swept over the captive's face did nothing to mar its brilliant beauty. She made no attempt to struggle. But the appeal in her eyes made him feel like a wanton boy who has trapped a wild bird.

How lovely she was! Her body was so slender that unconsciously he relaxed his grip somewhat, fearing to hurt her. Her dress was far from glamorous. She wore a dark pullover, blue trousers and rubber-soled shoes. An electric torch was stuck in her waistband.

She made no reply—just watched him.

"So you are a thief as well?" He knew that he spoke unnaturally.

Indeed, already, he had no idea how he was going to see the thing through. Whatever she was—and there must be some profound mystery behind it all—he knew that he was incapable of handing her over to the police.

"I am not a thief." It was a mere whisper. She was fighting pitiably for composure. "I swear to you I have taken nothing from here. Will you believe me?"

"Then why did you come?" A sense almost of nausea claimed him, as he visualized her clinging to that frail ladder. "You risked your life, as well as—"

"I am not afraid of heights. I was born in Grenoble. Besides, I had a safety line."

McKeigh suddenly remembered that on his one former meeting with this unique criminal she had used broken English.

"You have lost your accent rather suddenly!"

The ghost of a smile lighted the blue eyes. "You frightened me. I forgot! I speak good English if I speak naturally. Oh, I am an impostor. What use to deny it? But what I have done I had to do—"

"You mean, against your will?"

He was weakening; knew that he was weakening; and hated himself. He was seeking for any excuse to condone the conduct of his prisoner. But he continued to hold her fast.

She shook her head, so that light danced entrancingly in her wavy hair. "I believe in the right of what I do, if not always in the way I have to do it. I simply obey orders."

"Whose orders? Sumuru?"

"I never heard that name. No, someone who is a genius. One day you may know how great a genius—when the world is saved from another war."

28

Tony McKeigh knew that he was adoring her with his eyes, for a flush swept over her pale face and she lowered her lashes. He knew that he was lost, but he didn't know what to do about it. He sought refuge in words.

"But why should you, a girl, be sent on such a hazardous business?"

"What I came to do was—highly confidential."

"Then you are a senior rating, so to speak? But you swore you had taken nothing."

"I *have* taken nothing. I swear it again. And now—"

She raised her lashes, and Tony McKeigh bathed in the blue lagoon of her eyes. "Let me go! I beg of you, I entreat you—let me go! Listen, for a moment. You know I am an impostor, a criminal if you like, but in this I am sincere. She foresees everything. You are playing with death if you refuse me. Please, please, let me go!"

She grasped the lapels of his coat. Her eyes were imploring. And, even as he hesitated, their expression changed. They were focused beyond him, into the apartment at his back. And he read horror there.

Suddenly, she cried out—and her words were not addressed to *him...*

"No! *no,* I say! It is My Lady's order!" Then, addressing McKeigh, but not once diverting that set stare: "Don't move! Don't look behind you!"

For the first time, so strongly had emotion claimed him, he heard a furtive movement.

There was someone else in the room!

"Go back and wait for me. I can take care of myself."

Tony McKeigh held his breath. A conviction had come that his life hung in the scales. He visualized some sub-human creature who had come silently down the ladder—-a creature armed with death in a dreadful form—creeping stealthily towards him.... Again, he detected faint stirrings.

Those frightened eyes were watching some slowly-moving figure. Then, they were raised again to his own. Colour had fled from the girl's cheeks.

"Try to understand!" she whispered. "I have only to raise my voice and, for you, it would be finished! I have burned a photograph. The ashes are in that basket. Give me your word. Stay here for five minutes. Don't use the phone. Then—do as you like. *Please,* promise!"

It *was force majeure.* He was glad. This was his way out.

"I promise," he said huskily. "But—"

III

Sister Viola sat before Our Lady making her report. She had changed into the plain frock which she had worn earlier.

Madonna, also, had altered her dress. She was no longer an odalisque. She wore a blue, trousered suit and a dark pullover.

Seated in a high-back armchair of carved, blackened oak, her elbows rested on a narrow oak table littered with books and documents and lighted by a lamp on an Ancient Egyptian bronze pedestal. There was no other lamp in the room, a small library, so that My Lady showed framed in shadows. A silk scarf covered her hair, and a mink cloak lay over the back of her chair, suggesting either that she proposed to go out or that she had just come in.

Now, the golden voice broke a long silence.

"You have done well, Viola. One of our friends has occupied an apartment above Mr. Roscoe since his arrival in the city. I was uncertain if his business was with *me* until this evening. But I knew he was dangerous, and had to be watched. The man on duty in the hotel lobby knows him by sight, but, unfortunately, not his friend. And so, you were nearly caught?"

"Very nearly, My Lady! Sanchez saw—the other man— look out of the window, and came down at once."

"That was his duty. But I am thinking, Viola... This other man. Are you sure he didn't mention his name when you gave the wallet to him earlier to-night?"

Viola bit her lip.

"He did, My Lady. I think it was McKeigh."

Madonna grew even more thoughtful.

"McKeigh? ... I wonder what the association can be? You were quite right, of course, in checking Sanchez. He is too fond of harsh methods. The discovery of a body in the apartment might have had unfortunate consequences." Long lashes were raised. My Lady cast a searching glance at Viola. "You made sure that the negative was destroyed?"

"Yes, Madonna. Both the negative and the print."

"It is lucky they were shown to our friend, Lady Arling, and the name mentioned of the man to whom they were being sent. Her cable enabled us to act in time, as well as pointing to the identity of The Major..."

IV

"Your drivelling sentimentality," Drake Roscoe told Tony, "will be *my* finish! That blue-eyed acrobat must be a star in Sumuru's circus, and you play Romeo when you ought to be handling her with a club!"

His rapid conversation at times reminded McKeigh of the rattle of a typewriter.

"Go slow, Roscoe! How could I?"

Lieutenant Cody, who had driven Roscoe back, grunted sympathetically. "Takes years of experience to give an easy-looker the K.O."

"Copies of that photograph would have been circulated from coast to coast. Only one in existence. Ah, well!" Drake Roscoe clapped his hand on McKeigh's shoulder. "At least it shows that I was right. We shall find that a guest in the apartment above mine left rather hurriedly to-night!"

McKeigh grinned wryly. "You see—"

"Forget it, Mac. I'm not blaming you. You only did what I should have done—with one of Sumuru's thugs standing behind me!"

And as he spoke, Tony McKeigh seemed to see again the scene in that shadowy warehouse, grotesque, macabre, the form of the petrified man outlined under oilskins beneath a solitary lamp, the shining badges of the police, and Drake Roscoe's grim face.

"Glance over that, Mac. As you're used to codes and signals I guess you can fill in the gaps."

Roscoe handed McKeigh the memo book found on the victim. It had been partially dried and was open at the only page containing writing. The writing was in soft pencil, and water had obliterated much of it. But this was what Tony made out:

"—believed to be—hulk *John P. F.*—off—Island—

"Sally—offered up—accept—torrow night.

"Have—C—confirm—

"Describe Ariosto—"

"What d'you make of it, Mac? Your guess should be at least as good as mine."

"Well—roughly this: Something, or somebody, believed to be on board a hulk called the *John P. F.*—"

"John P. Faraway!" Lieutenant Cody interrupted. "Could only be that. An old pilot boat anchored off the tip of Welfare Island. Nobody knows why. Maybe marks a wreck."

"Thanks! We're making headway. Then, it goes on 'Sally somebody—'"

"Obviously Sally Obershaw!" Roscoe said.

"Quite. Sally Obershaw is to be 'offered up'—whatever that may mean. It sounds horrible! Then we have the word 'accept,' a gap, and (evidently), 'to-morrow night.'"

Lieutenant Cody exchanged glances with Drake Roscoe.

"Has she fallen into the hands of some lunatic who goes in for human sacrifices, Mr. Roscoe?" he asked.

Drake Roscoe's expression was almost fierce.

"In one sense, yes. Sumuru has no scruples. But I don't believe—I don't dare to believe—that the girl's life is in danger." He turned to Tony McKeigh. "I read the next note to mean, 'Have *Celie* confirm.' She was evidently going to give evidence, when I arrived. And the last entry is clear enough—but cryptic. Someone—either Kerrigan or the woman—proposed to describe Ariosto. As I haven't the slightest idea who Ariosto may be, this just adds to the general confusion.

"Must be one of the gang," Cody muttered, glancing at his watch. "Time we started, sir."

"Where are we going?" Tony McKeigh asked.

"I'm going to look over the hulk, *John P. Faraway,"* Roscoe told him. "It's a foul and foggy night. Want to come along?"

"I wouldn't miss it for all the gold in Fort K.!"

V

Sea fog encroached more and more. The criss-cross of ships' masts and funnels, a nocturne of smoke-stacks and ragged outlines of undeveloped projects, faded ghost-like as the patrol-boat drew away from shore. Above and beyond lay an implication of vast masses, where lights blinked as if suspended in space or upon an overhanging mountainside. It became curiously quiet out on the water, a belt of silence over which the song of Manhattan passed in a whisper. Mingling with the sound of the propeller and hum of traffic on the bridge, McKeigh could hear a clang of distant bells, the more remote hoarse roar of a liner's whistle, borne on the ocean breeze.

Somewhere astern a fire burned fitfully, its red glare leaping up, fading away, behind the muslin curtain of the sea fog...

The outline of a steamer, a phantom ship, materialized, loomed over them, and disappeared. Drake Roscoe began to speak. The midnight mystery of East River had claimed him. He spoke in a low voice, as if thinking aloud. The rest of the party had fallen silent...

"I don't like that reference to 'offering up'. In fact, I should fear the worst if I didn't know that Sumuru is thoroughly practical, if spectacular. She's a collector of beauty, and Sally Obershaw is an acknowledged beauty. She's also a collector of capital—and Sally's father is a multi-millionaire..."

"Quiet, sir!" came softly. The engine was shut off. "Hulk dead ahead. See her riding lights? What orders?"

"Run straight alongside—"

Drake Roscoe stopped abruptly.

From out of the mist came the zoom of a powerful motor. It rose to a tremendous crescendo, then faded—faded—upstream. The police craft began to roll in a heavy backwash.

"Have that damned speedboat intercepted, if possible!" Roscoe roared. The radio operator got feverishly busy. "Put me alongside! Jump to it!... But I'll swear we're too late!"

And the silence aboard the old pilot boat increased his fears. It was a silence broken only by the fretful whining of an anchor chain. As the police, rifles and machine guns at the ready, scrambled on to her dirty deck, suspicion became certainty.

The hulk was deserted.

But when the boarding party burst into the cabin and flooded it with their powerful lights, a scene so completely unexpected was revealed that Tony McKeigh pulled up with a jerk behind Roscoe, stifling an exclamation.

This wasn't the cabin of a scrapped pilot boat. It was an elegantly appointed miniature suite worthy of the *Queen Mary!*

"Hell!" Lieutenant Cody remarked. "What's this?"

"It's something," Drake Roscoe said between clenched teeth, "that's going to take a lot of explaining by the responsible authority!"

Here were a satin-covered divan, a Louis Quinze escritoire, Persian rugs, portholes curtained with Chinese silk. Beyond, they found a tiny but perfectly equipped bedroom; and an up-to-date shower-bath adjoined it. The suite was permeated by a faint but pleasant perfume. The closet contained no garments, and there were no papers in the bureau.

Roscoe turned to Lieutenant Cody.

"We shall need fingerprints and photographs. Take care of it. Check the history of this hulk. If somebody bought it, find out who did. Find out why it was allowed to lie here. Stir up the Marine Division. Wasn't it *anybody's* business to inspect this craft? Seems to me it could have been loaded with atom bombs and nobody the wiser!"

"Sally was *here!*" Tony McKeigh said excitedly. "This is where Sally Obershaw was hidden! Sumuru must have spotted that her thugs had muffed it when they didn't strip Lew Kerrigan. This damsel works fast!"

Roscoe's face seemed to grow haggard as he glanced at his watch. It registered 4 a.m.

"At any time after twelve hours from now, Sally Obershaw is to be 'offered up'—and I have to see her father at eight o'clock..."

CHAPTER FOUR

I

William Obershaw paced to and fro across the study floor. Early morning, and he hadn't been to bed all night. He was too restless to remain still for more than a few minutes at a time. His normally florid face had a leaden tinge, and he continually opened and then reclenched his muscular hands.

His grey hair retained traces of the golden red colour for which his daughter was celebrated, and a coloured photograph of Sally Obershaw stood on the big desk, at which he was forever glancing with an expression near one of despair. Except for the faint sound of his steps on the thick rug, the room, the whole penthouse apartment, remained strangely silent.

Drake Roscoe sat in a leathern armchair, scanning the pages of a book delicately bound in cream calf, upon which appeared in Oriental bold lettering the title, *Tears of Our Lady.*

"It took a long time to find, Mr. Roscoe. No doubt Sally had deliberately hidden the thing. But her mother found it in her room and I thought you should see it."

"Deceptive title," Roscoe muttered. "Far from a work of devotion. I should have to study it closely, of course." He examined the book with curiosity. "No publisher's imprint."

William Obershaw groaned. "I read French with difficulty, but I'd call it disgustingly obscene."

"I can't agree with you, Mr. Obershaw. A brief reading suggests that, as in the verses of Omar Khayyam, a deeper meaning underlies the words. There is a reference (as I told you) to this strange work in the dossier from Scotland Yard, which I haven't found time to digest entirely, yet."

"That was what set us to searching. Tell me"—he pulled up, opened and closed his hands— "do you believe, as man to man, Sally's alive?"

Roscoe took up a letter which lay beside him on a table.

"I have compared this with other writing of your daughter, Mr. Obershaw, and you yourself are prepared to swear that Sally wrote it. What object could she have had except that of relieving your anxiety?"

"I don't know. You're not encouraging me with false hopes? My wife is prostrated. But I'd rather stay silent than——"

Roscoe jumped up and laid his hand on the distraught man's shoulder.

"On my honour, Mr. Obershaw, I don't believe for a moment that your daughter's life is in danger. But she may have chosen a strange path, as others have done before her. Where that path leads, I can't tell you."

William Obershaw dropped wearily on to a sofa.

"I'm quite worn out. I wanted, and I still want, to offer a reward—one that would tempt any man, or any woman. I promised a huge fee to Lew Kerrigan when he called me. His awful death, which you have reported, seems to point to something worse, something bigger, than mere blackmail. This woman, in whose place you were to meet, must have been involved?"

"No doubt about it. If there's any clue on the Celie Artz premises, I assure you it will be found. The public offer of a reward, Mr. Obershaw, might lead to just the thing I don't want to happen—"

"What's that?"

"The removal of your daughter to some distant place."

"Good God!"

"There have been other cases of mysterious disappearances, as you know. In some of these, such rewards were offered... but not one has been claimed!"

William Obershaw stood up again, resumed his pathetic parade.

"I must trust *someone.* If you truly believe that Sally's alive, I leave it to you to act as you think best. I have told you that she's a girl of strong character, of almost alarming independence—in thought and action. She's very pretty, and she has brushed off more suitors than I could count. Also, some day she'll come into money.... Do you think *that's* the explanation?"

Drake Roscoe put *Tears of Our Lady* in his pocket, and frowned thoughtfully.

"It may have a bearing on the matter, Mr. Obershaw, but the influence of the extraordinary woman whom I know now, for certain, to be responsible for your daughter's disappearance, is the chief factor. We know her only as Sumuru. Her motives I have yet to learn. Whatever they are, I wish I could lay my hands on her ..."

The phone buzzed. William Obershaw dashed to his desk.

"Yes—yes! Speaking.... Yes, he's here right now." He turned to Roscoe, a light of hope in his eyes. "For you."

Roscoe's heavy brows were raised. He was wondering how many people knew that he had called on William Obershaw so early. He took up the instrument.

"Drake Roscoe here."

"Good morning, Major Roscoe," a woman's voice replied, a deliciously caressing voice, golden-toned. "I hoped I should find you there. I have just two things to say, until we meet—which I trust will be soon. The first is, tell Mr. Obershaw not to worry about Sally. She is in splendid health and spirits. She spent nearly a week on the water, you know, and looks as fresh as a spring flower...."

Drake Roscoe swallowed hard, then clenched his teeth.

"Did you say something, Major Roscoe?" the golden voice inquired.

"No."

"Secondly, please don't make the silly mistake so many others have made of trying to treat me as an ordinary criminal. I'm not, you know. The English agent who made things so difficult for me in London was just as obstinately truculent. I could quite easily have—what's the word Stalin likes?—liquidated him. But that's so vulgar, isn't it? I hate common men and adore clever ones. Please reassure Mr. Obershaw about Sally...."

There was a faint click, and the beautiful voice ceased. Roscoe hung up. He turned to William Obershaw.

"Yes—yes! News?"

"News. Sally is alive and well—"

"Thank God! Thank God! But—are you *sure?* Who was that speaking?"

"I'm quite sure. Don't ask me why. But I am."

"Who was the caller?"

"It was Sumuru..."

II

Tony McKeigh joined Drake Roscoe for breakfast in his hotel apartment. Following a wet and foggy night, the morning was sparkling in sunshine. Manhattan has an unpredictable climate. When the waiter had taken the orders and gone:

"First," Tony said, "the big story has been killed."

"What's that?"

"Some Higher Power, speaking through the Police Department, ordained that the deaths of Celie Artz and Lew Kerrigan should be reported, simply, as a love tragedy. So our newsroom tells me. No details re the state of the bodies to be printed. What about the Coroner? Or have you done away with coroners in the United States?"

"No. But that can be dealt with, too, in the public interest. You see, Mac, this thing might have caused a panic. I was wrong when I decided to release the story."

"But who's the Higher Power—the H.P. who corked the same?"

"Sorry, Mac—but I'm the H.P.! You see, I have been given very unusual facilities by Washington—almost *carte blanche*—to deal with this awful menace. And I have learned quite a bit from Scotland Yard's experience. I'm hoping to tempt another M.D., or the same, maybe, to declare these deaths due to *rigor Kubus.*"

"What good will that do?"

"This much—it will prove that Sumuru has established an identical set-up in Manhattan. If she's going to run true to form, we'll get her!"

"True to form—h'm! I fear, my dear Holmes, you play the horses."

Drake Roscoe lighted a cigar. "Could be." A real deep-sea stomach—which I never acquired. My first pipe is *after* the ham and eggs. Any report from the experts analysing poor Celie's premises?"

Roscoe snapped off his lighter, shook his head.

"Not a thing. It was a branch office of Sumuru's—and Sumuru rarely leaves clues."

"Lew Kerrigan's note-book?"

"An oversight—promptly corrected. Sally Obershaw was rushed away from the hulk before we had time to get there! Mac, this woman is a genius!"

"Marine Department report re hulk to hand?"

"Yes—by phone, ten minutes ago. The *John P. Faraway* was purchased, at scrap price, nearly a year back, by the Orson Shipbuilding Corporation for a client who planned to convert her to a sea-going yacht. Meanwhile, she was allowed to lie to her old moorings. Being private property, she was nobody's business."

"Name of client to hand?"

Drake Roscoe took his cigar from between his teeth and grinned at Tony McKeigh.

"You're in the wrong job, Mac. I wish you'd take over from me! The answer is—*no*. But that piece of information can't be long delayed. We have the day before us to find out where Sally Obershaw is to be 'offered up'—and not one ghost of a clue."

"Poor girl. Isn't it at least on the cards that she's defunct?"

"No!" Roscoe snapped out the word. "She's alive. She was on that hulk up to five minutes, or less, of our arrival. I don't know if she's a willing disciple of Sumuru, or if she's a prisoner; but I do know she's alive."

"And who imparted this spot of vital news?"

"Sumuru!"

Tony McKeigh sat back, open-mouthed.

"Sumuru?"

"Herself! She called me at William Obershaw's this morning. She has the sublime audacity of a truly dangerous character. I'm telling you again—Sumuru is a genius. I shall have to be a bigger man than I think I am to stand up to her. My sympathies are all with Scotland Yard and the British Secret Service. Sumuru is something unique in criminal history."

Tony McKeigh took out his pipe, then put it back again.

"Is she amusing to talk to?"

"Mac, she has the most wonderful voice I ever heard. It's magnetic, compelling and beautiful. She had me enthralled while she spoke. That woman could hypnotize all the people you could get into the Metropolitan Opera House, packed to the roof, by just talking to them!"

"After which, no doubt, selected attendants would step around and give everybody a shot *of rigor Kubus.* "

"You'd be less frivolous, Mac, if you'd spoken to her. This woman is formidable. Her record proves it. She's a dangerous fanatic of some kind—-and a fanatic is the toughest kind of opponent."

The waiter came in with breakfast.

"Where, and at what hour," Roscoe whispered to Tony McKeigh, "is Sally Obershaw to be 'offered up'?"

"Probably in some secret lair far from the madding crowd, somewhere miles away," Tony whispered back.

III

At this season there were many social activities in smarter Manhattan. International notabilities were numerous, among these the Duchesse de Severac, said to be the best-dressed woman in Paris. The Duchesse was a guest at the Finelander home in Greenwich, Connecticut, now kept up by the only surviving relative of the fabulously wealthy John J. Finelander. This was his daughter, Rhoda, a confirmed spinster, feminist, and invalid.

The Duchesse de Severac, one of Europe's leading theosophists, had many American disciples, and she had expressed a wish to address a number of these (all women) before returning to Paris. Rhoda Finelander had volunteered, enthusiastically, to arrange the meeting, and had put the old Finelander town home in New York at the Duchesse's disposal for the purpose.

As the huge mansion, now a showplace, was open to the public during part of every week, it was decided that the affair should take place at night, admission to be by invitation only. Even the guards of the magnificent Finelander collection would be banished to the lobbies.

The Duchesse de Severac would speak at midnight.

Publicity, she insisted, must at all costs be avoided. And so those fortunate enough to receive invitations were bidden to come at various times between eleven and eleven-forty-five, and to present their cards at the private entrance in the street at the back of the great building. Refreshments would be served in the suite reserved for the family, upstairs.

No awning was put out. No special police were on duty. If a passing patrolman had noted an unusual number of cars and taxis pulling up before the door he would have concluded merely that an after-opera reception, or something of the sort, was being given in the Finelander apartment.

Of course, a really astute officer might have noted that all the guests were women, and he could, then, hardly have failed to observe that they were, without exception, very pretty women.

The former dining room of the Finelander mansion, sometimes used for concerts of chamber music, the Duchesse had rejected as unsuitable. She would address her disciples in the beautiful covered court known as the Roman atrium. This had a marble pool in the centre, set amid banks of flowers. Surrounding it were pillars and cloisters on a slightly higher level, in which, to-night, seats had been provided for the guests.

One end of the rectangular court had been curtained off. The draperies were of a pale rose colour.

At ten minutes to twelve, all the guests had been ushered to their places by remarkably attractive girls wearing white Grecian robes. Every door communicating with the atrium was locked, and an expectant hush fell upon the beautiful audience.

It was broken, very sweetly, by a wave of music played upon harps, and the soft singing of a hidden female choir. The music swelled up, fell, died away; swelled up again, and faded.

Followed a moment of complete silence. Then the rose draperies were parted, which produced a sound like that of fairy bells. The Duchesse stood there, smiling.

Like her chosen attendants, she wore a white Grecian robe. It was fastened on one snowy shoulder by an emerald brooch, and its graceful folds rippled around her figure so that she seemed to be draped in gleaming gossamer. A gold net confined her hair. She stood statuesquely still, holding a white peacock fan.

Every woman in the atrium dropped to her knees. A sound, a whisper, a prayer, no more than a concerted sigh, swept around the pillared court.

"Our Lady!"

The Duchesse scattered phantom kisses with both hands.

"Rise up, dear children. Resume your seats. It is rarely that I have the happiness of seeing so many lovely faces, of looking into so many loyal eyes. All of you here to-night are hierophants dedicated to the great cause. Some belong to one of my households, some to the schools. Others work independently, but effectively, in the coarse outside world."

She swayed the white fan with indolent grace. No sound came from her listeners. They had fallen under the spell of that exquisite voice.

"Deformed brains are permitted to inflame the fools of the world. Men like rats creep out of the sewers which bred them and spread plague amongst those who once were clean. Such sewer rats are in our midst to-day, poisoning our children, polluting the very air we breathe.... They must be destroyed, or driven back to their sewers. In this task, every one of you has a part."

As the speaker's eyes, so shadowed by heavy lashes that no one could have defined their colour, swept a slow glance around the assembly, that hushed sigh arose again.

41

"Our Lady ..."

"Beauty, properly used, is power. Beauty must take the place of ugliness. Our Order controls more beauty, and therefore has greater secret power, than any society the world has known. By means of this we command some of the greatest intellects in the spheres of art, science and politics; for men, however brilliantly gifted, readily become enslaved by beauty. We have gone far. But we have to go farther yet. We failed to remove in time the ugliness which brought about the World War—but we did much to frustrate it. We inspired the madness which destroyed the man Hitler. This time, we dare not fail. We must strike first."

The four last words rose to a bell note, a challenge. It was answered by a fervid murmur.

"Woman, once called the Vessel, is in fact the spring from which flow beauty and power. That emblem of the coiled serpent which everyone here bears upon her body, is a proud crest. Whilst women move in silence, seemingly supine, their influence is exercised unnoticed. When women are forced to strike, the stroke is fatal."

The murmur, now, framed words—fervid, emotional:

"Our Lady!"

Our Lady smiled triumphantly, and swept the white fan around to include all in a graceful gesture.

"We are here to welcome—if you approve my choice—a new sister to our Order. She is of worthy birth. She is cultured and wealthy. She renounces much in joining us. At her own request, she was granted a week's retreat during which to settle any doubts which remained. Of her beauty, you are here to be the judges."

The Duchesse turned. The space behind her was draped and shadowy. A high, sweet note sounded—that of a silver bell—and Sally Obershaw came in.

She resembled a lovely nude statue tinted by a master artist to reproduce the warm hues of flesh. Her glorious hair framed her face in red-golden fire.

Her composure was unruffled. She advanced proudly, but without arrogance, to face the jury of her peers. The ordeal called "offering up", found her calm. The Duchesse touched Sally's shoulder with her fan.

"Is she worthy of us? Do you accept her?"

And a response came which left no room for doubt:

"We do, Madonna!"

As the new Sister retired through the draperies, hidden harps and voices rose in a triumphant chant, and the rose-coloured curtains were closed upon the Duchesse, smiling and wafting kisses to her enthralled disciples....

CHAPTER FIVE

I

ON the following night, when all Tony McKeigh's calls to the hotel got the same reply, "Mr. Roscoe doesn't answer," he began to feel really worried. He had inquired, personally, no less than five times during the day and had been told that Roscoe was out.

But he hadn't hurried away. He had explored every one of the public rooms, bars and restaurants, on each occasion. He hated to accept the idea that he was a victim of love at first sight, but certainly he had all the symptoms. Because he would have had to admit that he wasn't looking for Roscoe; he was looking for the girl with those wonderful blue eyes, the girl he had held in his arms, the girl whose name he didn't know.

Something, during that last meeting, when she had come as a thief, had struck a new note deep inside him. She was an associate of criminals, desperate, murderous criminals, and he should have hated and despised her. But he didn't.

On his last visit to the hotel, In late afternoon, he had noticed a dangerous-looking half-caste, very well dressed, who seemed to be watching him. He had wondered if his behaviour had aroused the suspicion of the chief house detective, and if the dusky man might be one of his staff.

He had left, hurriedly, by the Park Avenue door, and had had a glimpse, just stepping out of a Hispano-Suiza, of one of the most elegantly beautiful Frenchwomen he had ever seen. As she swept in, escorted by a doorman as royalty is escorted, he decided that she must be some new screen actress. She passed so close to him, throwing back the collar of her mink coat as she came to the entrance, that Tony's keen observant eye registered a curious fact. Her ear, which resembled a pink shell, had an unusual formation. There was no lobe. It was like the ear of a faun. A faint, unfamiliar perfume breathed momentarily on the air—and she was gone.

But he reflected that he would have been notified of the arrival of any theatre celebrities from overseas, and was moving off, when he heard a woman say to her friend, in tones of hushed adoration, "Isn't the Duchesse divine?"

"Is she a duchess, dear? I didn't know."

"The Duchesse de Severac, the best-dressed woman in Paris..."

But that memory had soon faded. He hadn't even troubled to check up the Duchesse in his French *Who's Who*. He was absorbed by other memories. And they grew more poignant, more important, all the time. Would he ever look again into those glorious blue eyes?

Now, here he was with the night on his hands, keen to rejoin Drake Roscoe for the sheer excitement of the job which had brought him to Manhattan. But Roscoe was out of contact. The girl whose bewitching face was always before him, belonged to the inscrutable woman called Sumuru. Yet Tony told himself that if he had known where to look for Sumuru...

What?

He began to fill his pipe. What would he have done? Gone along and asked her if he might have a chat with a friend of hers who had blue eyes and a mass of chestnut hair?

Tony decided to walk to the club and find somebody sane to talk to.

It was a beautiful, clear night, with a quarter moon in a cloudless sky—an ideal night for romance. He paused for a moment as he came out, looking up at the stars. Then, he looked right and left along the street.

Only two people were in sight—a man going east and a girl going west.

Tony McKeigh caught his breath. It wouldn't be the first time since that encounter in Drake Roscoe's apartment that he had nearly made a fool of himself. But, this time, surely he couldn't be mistaken?

She wore no hat, and as she walked slowly past a lighted window he saw the gleam of that marvellous hair. She wore a shaped, light coat, and her figure, her carriage were unmistakable. Taking fantastically long strides, Tony McKeigh knocked out his pipe and set off to put the matter to the test.

He had only a short distance to go, and as he drew alongside she glanced quickly up at him.

It was she!

Before he could find words, the delightful idea sprang to his mind that she had come to look for him! Surely it was more than a coincidence—an answer to a prayer?

When he found words, they were tame enough, considering his inward excitement:

"Hullo! It's nice to see you!"

Those lovely eyes looked into his again. Their expression chilled him. It was one of dreadful unhappiness.

"I'm afraid you frightened me, Mr. McKeigh."

"But you're glad to see me, I hope? I was afraid I should never *see you* any more."

She continued to walk along, now looking straight ahead.

"I can't think why you should want to see me—unless to hand me over to the police."

"Please don't say that." He held her arm, very gently. "I know you were taking frightful chances and that anything might have happened. But I'm perfectly sure you believed you were acting in a good cause. Perfectly certain of it. Secret agents take frightful chances every day, because they believe in their job."

She didn't answer for a moment, and then:

"If I say that I *am* glad to see you again"—she spoke in a low voice— "will you do something that may seem very strange—just to make me happy?"

"Only give it a name!"

"Start calling for a policeman!"

Tony pulled her up, turned her, and looked into her face.

"Say that again."

"Call for a policeman. But let me slip away before it's too late."

The blue eyes looked unflinchingly into his own. (How lovely she was!) This wasn't a jest. She meant it!

"You mean"—Tony McKeigh's voice was none too steady— "you want me to *pretend* to have you arrested, but to make sure you're not?"

"Yes. I mean just that. It will be better for you, and better for me." He noted, even in his feverish frame of mind, that her speech had no trace of accent. "Will you do it—for *my* sake?"

Tony McKeigh held her in a firm grip.

"No! For your sake, I won't do anything so mad. If I wanted to have you arrested, the simple way would be to take you back to my apartment and call the police. I shouldn't have to make a scene out here on the street!"

She kept on watching him steadily.

"There's no other way—for me, or for you. Otherwise, you will force me to do something I hate to do. I can escape quite easily, if you will let me ... I have a car at the end of the block."

Yet, even now, so deep was his infatuation, Tony McKeigh didn't begin to understand; or, if the truth was dawning dimly, he rejected it. She had a car at the corner! His heart leapt. She *had* come to look for him!

"Suppose we walk back to my apartment and just talk this thing over, quietly?"

An expression strangely like despair shadowed the blue eyes.

"You don't know what you ask—what it will mean."

"There are no strings to it. I just want to talk to you. I owe something to Roscoe, and he'll want to know why I didn't hold you—if I don't."

"Very well. You leave me no choice."

As she turned to go back:

"You know my name," Tony said. "But I don't know yours."

There was a momentary hesitation, and then:

"My name is Viola Stayton," she answered, quietly.

"Then you are not French?"

"No. I was educated in France, where I was born. I am English—like you."

"Strictly speaking, Irish—but it's near enough."

He felt like singing with happiness as he put his key in the street door and led Viola to the elevator. It had happened. A dream had come true. It rested with him, now, to play his cards well ...

II

Our Lady sat before a Buhl escritoire, one rounded elbow resting on the open desk. She was listening to someone speaking on the phone. She wore full evening dress and her perfect shoulders gleamed like white satin in the subdued light.

"I understand, Caspar," she said. "He is a man of good educational background. But what of his family?"

Her long lashes drooping drowsily, she listened again for a while.

"In brief," she murmured presently, "what is called sound yeoman stock, in England. So far, very well. We must not act hastily. Has Sanchez reported?... They have gone in? There was no struggle?... Philo is here, yes. I shall be waiting for the call ...."

III

Tony McKeigh, at about this time, returned from the kitchenette, where he had gone for ice, and mixed himself a drink. Viola had declined one.

"It's just on the cards," he told her, "that I don't quite get the picture."

But his eyes were glued to the picture—the picture of Viola as she sat watching him, in his own living-room: a dream come to life. She had removed her coat (at his pressing invitation) and wore a plain blue evening frock which left her rounded arms bare. He was imagining what the touch of those arms would be like against his cheeks, the intoxication of burying his face in that cloud of hair.

His facetious tone was forced. If ever he had wanted to be serious, this was the moment. But he was too highly tensed to trust himself. Viola's calm, he sensed, was as artificial as his own.

She smiled, slightly but not happily.

"Yet it's very simple. You have asked me, and I have told you more than once, that I am glad to see you again. But, however I may feel about it, for us to be friends is just impossible."

"Nothing is impossible."

"That would be. You have seen what I am called upon to do for Our Lady——"

"You've used that expression before. As you're clearly not a domestic worker, I don't follow—unless you use the term in its religious sense."

Viola's glance dropped for a moment.

"I don't use it—in that sense. It is the name of the head of the Order to which I belong."

Tony, just in time, checked an impulse to add, "the Order which goes in for murder and abduction." Instead, he said:

"My dear girl, just plain common sense must tell you that this 'Order' will end up in Sing Sing. If—which is what I believe—you've been tricked into joining some underground movement, think again. You must know the thing is criminal. You have a conscience. 'Our Lady' will finish in a very hot chair!"

Viola was watching him again. She shook her head. The waves of her hair seemed to throw out sparks of light. Tony took a drink.

49

"You don't understand. But that can never happen. And I was not tricked into joining the Order. I was given plenty of time to make up my mind. Difficult things have to be done—things hard to understand. But, except for this, we are free to do as we please, except—"

"Except what?"

An expression swept across Viola's face and was gone so swiftly, that only a close observer would have detected it. But it encouraged Tony McKeigh to change his seat for one beside Viola on the settee.

"Viola—I'm called Tony—I'm afraid I am going to make a complete fool of myself. Because I don't know any more than the man in the moon who you are or where you come from. But, all the same, I'm going to fall madly in love with you!"

She seemed to shrink away as he placed his arm lightly around her shoulders.

"Don't, please don't—make love to me!"

"No." He drew his arm back. "It isn't fair. You really had no choice about coming here. I won't play dirty, Viola. But if you don't positively hate me, you can arrange another meeting, of your own free will. I *can* make love to you, then, without feeling a cad!"

Viola turned to him as he spoke, and her lovely eyes spoke a language so different from her words, that human nature conquered chivalry. Tony held her in his arms through a long, breathless kiss that seemed to transport him to an unknown world ...

When, at last, he recovered sanity, he released her with a sense of having behaved like an outsider. She was trembling.

"Viola! Viola, dear! You are angry. You have every right—

She didn't look at him.

"I am not angry. Everything is my fault. But what I do I have to do. You had at least a chance to let me go. You don't understand what has happened—what it means to me... what it is going to mean to you."

Tony couldn't trust himself, yet. He crossed to his desk, finished his drink and took up his pipe, which he had laid there when he came in with Viola.

"Please don't—"

He turned. Viola was watching him. Her expression was wild.

"My dear! Don't what?"

50

She swallowed, emotionally.

"Don't hate me for what I am—for what I have to do!"

"*Hate* you!"

He turned away again, stuffed tobacco into the bowl and lighted his pipe. The enigma of Viola's behaviour was beyond him. She had returned his kisses, but at the same time had given him the impression that he was violating a nun. He sat down beside her again, took her hand.

"You see I don't understand, Viola. Won't you try to make me understand?"

Viola was still trembling. She avoided looking at him.

"I shall *have* to try, now, sooner or later."

It was a mere whisper. Whatever could she mean? Sooner or later...

He didn't speak at once, but found himself considering those words— "Sooner or later."

What was it Roscoe had said? Something about "she belongs to Sumuru and so she can never belong to anybody else." But he would prove that Roscoe was wrong about that.

"Sooner or later...." He loved her soft voice, could listen to it for ever.

He had dropped his pipe. Viola had stooped to pick it up.

"Sooner or later...."

What was the matter with him? There seemed to be a mist in the room.... Viola's soft arms were around his neck... her lips clung to his....

He could still hear those words, like an endless echo:

"Sooner... or... later..."

"Sooner ..."

"Or later...."

There was a brief moment of fear, of doubt. What had happened? Was he dying? Could it be...

IV

He was floating in space like a captive balloon. A thin silken cord held him moored to earth. He could look down—down—down—right to where this cord ended. And it ended up on his own body, which lay slumped on the settee in his own living-room!

There was no sense of fear; just an acceptance of the fact that he was dead, that he was a spirit looking down upon the body from which life had fled. Soon, very soon, the cord would break, and then he would be free to soar upward, untroubled by those limitations of the flesh which, now, he realized he had always hated.

A woman was bending over the body on the settee. She seemed to be examining it very closely. She wore a long fur cloak. Of course! she must be a woman doctor who had happened to be available in the emergency of his sudden seizure.

But he wondered why there was no one else in the room. Where was Viola? Perhaps she had gone out to admit the ambulance man.

Viola.... There had been something in his mind about Viola just in that last moment before the blank came, some Question to which he couldn't find an answer.

The woman in the cloak stood upright. She seemed to be listening. He could see her face, at last. Why, of course (he accepted the discovery, like everything else, without alarm, without surprise), it was the Duchesse de Severac. He saw her stoop to his body. She seemed to be raising his head. What was she doing? Forcing something between his teeth?

Then—she had gone, and—

The silken cord was tightening, dragging him down, dragging him back—and he didn't want to go!

He fought against the remorseless pull, but it wouldn't snap, it wouldn't slacken. It had him right back beside his own dead body, now, and he struggled so convulsively that it seemed to become fastened around his throat. It was choking him! He couldn't breathe! His heart was bursting....

He made one final, desperate effort to throw off that strangling cord—and found himself upright on the settee!

There was a mist before his eyes, a moving mist. His head swam dizzily. But as the mist dispersed he made a curious discovery:

He wasn't dead. He was in his own room. And he was alone!

Where Viola had been seated, beside him, her coat thrown over the back of the couch, there was nothing. He could see an empty glass on the desk. His pipe lay beside it. He stood up, staggered slightly, then crossed unsteadily to the desk and picked up the pipe.

The bowl was empty—cold. Yet, surely he had been smoking at the moment of his seizure?

He looked at his watch.

He had been unconscious for nearly an hour!

Clenching his teeth and his fists, he stared all around. Nothing was out of place. Nothing had been disturbed.

A horrible explanation sprang to his mind. He had been temporarily mad! But when had madness begun? Where did reality end? Had he ever gone out—seen Viola—brought her back here? Or had the entire episode, first to last, been pure hallucination?

He dropped back on the settee, buried his face in his hands.

And it was as he sat there, fighting with despair, that he detected something.

It was very slight. Only, perhaps, in his hypersensitive condition could he have noticed it.

A faint, exquisite perfume.

Viola had not used it. Yet—he had met with it, somewhere, and recently, once before.

CHAPTER SIX

I

Our Lady was seated again beside the Buhl escritoire, sideways in a gilded chair. Her elbow rested on the open desk her mink cloak was thrown over the back of the chair.

Viola knelt on a cushion at her feet.

"I have seen him, child. You seem strangely disturbed. Tell me why."

The sweet voice was like healing music. Viola looked up with tears in her eyes.

"It frightened me, Madonna. When he was overcome, when he became unconscious. I felt that, perhaps, I had—"

"Go on, Viola. That perhaps you had what?"

"Killed him!" A whisper.

Sumuru's wonderful eyes looked down at the girl's bowed head.

"And this disturbed you? Why should it, Viola? He might have been one life standing in the way of happiness for many. It isn't true, in his case, as you know. Because you have never doubted my word. But there are such men—men who acquire power and use it to stifle beauty, joy, all the things that really matter to poor humanity. You know our philosophy, child. You would not hesitate to aid in the destruction of an Adolf Hitler, or of another who might embrace the Satanic creed he stood for?"

Viola shook her head.

"You know, Madonna, I should always obey—for Our Lady is always—wise."

Sumuru stooped and stroked the gleaming hair.

"Tell me, Viola, did you have any trouble in inducing him to return with you to his apartment?"

"No, Madonna."

"Is he in love with you?"

"He—said so."

"Did he make love to you?"

Viola nodded.

"You were not too harsh?"

"No, Madonna. I tried to obey your orders. It was impossible to put the grey powder in his glass. I put it in the bowl of his pipe. You said it could be smoked."

"It is tasteless in tobacco and very rapid in its action. Ariosto could make a great fortune with it. You emptied and cleaned the pipe?"

"Yes, Madonna—as you told me to empty and clean the glass, had I used one."

"Well—I came to your call, and I have seen him. He will have revived by now."

Viola clenched her hands so tightly that her nails hurt her palms.

"Yes, Madonna."

"He is not an impossible selection for our Order. But, unfortunately, he knows already that you belong to me. Any future meeting might be dangerous. He might learn too much. And there are several loyal friends of ours in many ways more suitable for you to mate with. This must be considered. What are your own inclinations, Viola?"

Viola's hands remained clenched.

"Always, Madonna, my inclinations are yours...."

II

Drake Roscoe had been inaccessible during this memorable day for a variety of reasons. One, that he had driven out fairly early to a charming little home near Wilton, Connecticut, to see (by appointment) Mark Donovan, formerly a war correspondent for the Alliance Press but now a free-lance writer.

Mark Donovan was the man who had helped Scotland Yard find the only photograph of the Marquise Sumuru. He had actually known this mysterious woman. His testimony made up a considerable part of the *dossier Sumuru* dispatched to Roscoe.

As the car drove in, Mark Donovan came down from the porch to welcome his visitor. Roscoe noted that he was a tall, dark and strikingly handsome fellow, with a winning smile and great simplicity of manner, almost shyness.

"Mr. Drake Roscoe, I'm happy to meet you—but sorry about the matter that brings you here. Before we join her—" Donovan tried to hide his embarrassment— "I want to ask you to keep all this business from Claudette, my wife. You see the very name of Sumuru affects her horribly. So—we never mention it."

He turned to go in, but Drake Roscoe checked him.

"Just one moment, Mr. Donovan. I'm sorry, too, in the circumstances. But, tell me—what is the cause of this uneasiness of

56

your wife's? I mean—does she fear this woman because of your past association with her, or—?"

Mark Donovan shook his head. He grasped Roscoe's arm in a muscular hand.

"No, sir. There's another reason. My wife, for some time, was in the power of Sumuru. I had the good luck to get her away. We're just as happy as two people could be. We figured we had left Sumuru behind us (if she was alive) when we sailed from Europe. Now—"

"I see. Then, until we can manage a few minutes alone together, I have a perfectly good explanation for my call. You know Tony McKeigh?"

"Tony McKeigh? Why, yes! I knew him in London. He went into the Navy. Is he here?"

"He's at the *Telegram's* New York office. He asked me to call when I happened to be this way, and here I am."

Donovan squeezed Roscoe's arm.

"Thanks for that. I'm obliged. Come right in."

Although prepared by what he had heard of Sumuru's women, Mrs. Mark Donovan still gave Roscoe a surprise. She was one of the loveliest girls he had ever met. A more striking couple would have been hard to find. Claudette was French, and altogether charming. She was clearly devoted to Mark Donovan, and he to her.

"This is Mr. Drake Roscoe, Claudette, who called me yesterday, remember? We have an old mutual friend, Tony McKeigh, another newspaperman, I used to know in London."

"I won't want to be a nuisance in any way, Mrs. Donovan," Roscoe assured her. "I just pulled in to say how-do to Mac's friend, as I was around this way."

"You are more than welcome. Mark will get drinks and lunch will be ready in half an hour."

"But really I feel an intruder—"

Mark nudged him, as Claudette went on, smiling, and then:

"After lunch," he whispered, "we can have a chat together in my workroom."

And then Drake Roscoe was taken to meet the third member of the family, Claudette II. He was no judge of babies, but if there was a prettier child than this violet-eyed, dimpled little creature anywhere in the world, he had never seen her. Claudette II promised to be a duplicate of her beautiful mother.

Claudette rejoined them for cocktails, and nothing was said about the business which had brought Roscoe out to Connecticut, all through luncheon. Roscoe detected at times a fleeting look of anxiety in Claudette's eyes. It seemed to come just when she was watching Mark, listening to him, smiling; in the very middle of her happiness. He wondered if she had doubts about so great a happiness lasting.

After lunch, she went to see to Claudette II, and Mark led the way to his little book-lined sanctum and settled his visitor in a comfortable armchair. The room was on the ground floor, and through the opened window Roscoe could see a well-kept garden backed picturesquely by a clump of silver birches.

"I haven't said a word to my wife," Mark Donovan began; "but I believe she knows, intuitively, that something's wrong. It turned me cold when you told me. What it would do to Claudette I hate to think. You are sure—definitely sure—that this woman is in America?"

"Quite sure, Mr. Donovan. In fact, she has spoken to me, on the phone."

Mark Donovan leaned forward, resting his chin in his hand. A cloud had settled upon him.

"I hoped—and I mean what I say—that that woman was dead. No one like her, in my opinion, has ever darkened the world before. She must be Satan's mistress."

"All I know of her is that she has a haunting voice. No doubt you can give me many details."

"Some maybe, yes. In the first place, perhaps I should say she's the most beautiful woman I ever saw—"

"I thought, Mr. Donovan, that your wife—"

"Claudette's a lovely girl, I know. But Sumuru is, well, indescribable—"

"Is she young?"

"She appears to be."

"Dark or fair?"

"No two accounts agree!"

"I know. But what's yours?"

"Honestly, I couldn't say. I never saw her without some sort of covering on her hair."

"But her eyes—her complexion?"

"She has very fair skin. I have no idea what colour her eyes are! She has a perfect figure. It's my honest opinion—although I know it sounds silly—that she's a sorceress! She can cast spells—with her voice, and with her eyes."

"Of which you don't know the colour!"

"This I believe is part of the sorcery. Because I'm not the only man who has met her and failed to describe her. Accounts agree only in one respect. She is dangerously beautiful."

"Helen of Troy returned to earth!"

"Odd you should say that, Mr. Roscoe. I heard an equally keen observer make just the same remark. Sumuru seems to possess the magic of appearing to every man as his ideal of feminine perfection. In other words, the World's Desire. Speaking from experience, I should doubt if there's a soul alive who could resist her witchcraft. As well as her infernal beauty she has the brains of any two men of genius."

Drake Roscoe gazed out of the window with unseeing eyes.

"Am I right in supposing, Mr. Donovan, that Sumuru believes the salvation of the world to be possible only if women rule it?"

"She told me so!"

"What would become of the men?" Only those with great physical beauty, and/or great brains, would survive. They would be mated with her selected women and so produce a perfect race."

Roscoe stood up, his back to the open window, and stared across at Mark Donovan.

"Has she many followers, do you think?"

"Thousands, I believe. And all over the world."

She must be much older than she appears to be."

"It would seem so, I agree."

"The offspring of these ideal unions would be trained from childhood in Sumuru's peculiar philosophy, I suppose?"

Mark Donovan nodded.

"As in Soviet Russia. My wife, of course, knows far more than I know. But we made a pact, right from the start, that we'd never talk about it."

"I understand. But now that Sumuru is here...."

There came a muffled cry. Mark Donovan sprang up. Roscoe turned.

Claudette, her face deathly pale, was staring in at the window.

III

"Oh, Mark! Mark! I felt it. I think I knew it. I have sensed *her* presence about me again, for a long while now—ever since the little one came."

Claudette lay back in the armchair from which Roscoe had stood up. Mark was beside her, his expression deeply anxious. But she made a great effort to win composure.

"I can't say how sorry I am," Roscoe declared. "Your husband had impressed it on me that you weren't to be told."

"I'm glad it happened," Claudette assured him. "I was passing the window on my way to join you when I heard *her* name."

"Will you tell me something, Mrs. Donovan?" Roscoe spoke gently. "Why, after this lapse of time, should you fear this woman? Were you tied to her in any way? Did you break any solemn vow when you—escaped?"

"No." Claudette's naturally lovely colouring was returning. She looked up at her husband. "I was not a member of the Order at all, although I had received some instruction.

"Madonna—" She checked herself, then shrugged in an oddly Gallic way. "That slipped out. They all called her Madonna. *She* particularly wanted me to join them, for some reason."

Drake Roscoe hesitated to put the next question, but at last:

"Don't bother to answer if it disturbs you in any way, Mrs. Donovan," he said. "But is there some sort of ceremony known as 'offering up'?"

Claudette nodded, glancing shyly at Mark.

"Yes. If the novice is accepted, she is enrolled in the Order."

"Suppose she isn't accepted?"

"I believe they all are. You see, their accomplishments, family history, health and so forth, are known to Our Lady (you call her Sumuru) before the 'offering up'. It just consists of"—she flushed— "showing herself to a committee of women of the Order."

"When you—ran away—from Sumuru, did she attempt to recapture you, Mrs. Donovan?"

Again, Claudette exchanged glances with her husband.

"Yes. She did!"

60

"And, having failed, did she try to interfere with your marriage?"

"No, sir," Mark Donovan broke in. "She said she hoped to be at the wedding—"

Claudette clutched his arm.

"She *was* there, Mark! I never told you before, but now I might as well. I saw her standing at the back of the church. She smiled at me!"

"I know at last," Mark said grimly, "why you nearly fainted as we came out!"

"I happen to be aware"—Roscoe spoke in a quiet voice— "that heavy penalties fall on any member of this Order who talks too much. Am I right in believing, Mrs. Donovan, that they carry an indelible tattoo mark—like the thugs of India?"

Claudette nodded unhappily.

"A snake with its tail in its mouth. It isn't tattooed. It is painted on the skin with some secret preparation. It's hardly visible. But it can't be removed."

There was a short, uneasy silence. Then Drake Roscoe spoke again.

As Sumuru seemed to approve your marriage, Mrs. Donovan, and has never taken any steps to disturb it, I can't see that you have anything to fear from her." Claudette raised her eyes, looked up at Roscoe.

"Our Lady plans a new world, Mr. Roscoe, a world peopled by those of her own choosing, Don't you see? Oh, Mark!" She clutched her husband wildly. "Can't you understand? My baby! my baby! She will try to get my baby...."

CHAPTER SEVEN

I

When Drake Roscoe returned to his hotel, late in the afternoon, he saw that Tony McKeigh had made several calls. But there was no reply from Tony's number. William Obershaw had called up, too, and there were police reports to be read.

Although Manhattan had been combed, throughout the night and all day, by the largest number of detectives ever assigned to one case, not a clue had come to hand to show where Sally Obershaw had been taken. There was, though, one report, from the Marine Division, which Roscoe read a second time.

It stated that the client on whose behalf the hulk *John P. Faraway* had been bought by the shipbuilding firm was Miss Rhoda Finelander, whose address was given as Greenwich, Conn. Roscoe swore under his breath. He might have called on Miss Finelander while he was so near to her home.

But the news gave him food for thought.

He understood, now, why the craft had remained anchored in the river, undisturbed. The influence of the family would be quite enough to explain this. The late John J. Finelander had been one of Manhattan's most distinguished and respected citizens. This deep respect his only daughter had inherited, as well as his vast estate. The Finelander Bequest to the Metropolitan Museum, the virtual present to the public (by Miss Rhoda) of the town mansion, these were patriotic gifts which New York City could never adequately reward.

Roscoe had to face a question, and find an answer to it:

Did Rhoda Finelander know how the *John P. Faraway* had been fitted out? If it had been done by her own orders, what was her object?

Roscoe made several calls, and learned that a large upstairs apartment was reserved in the town home for the use of the family. There was a resident housekeeper.

This happened to be one of the days on which the historic collection was closed to the public, and Drake Roscoe was directed by a man in uniform to apply at the private door on the adjoining street.

A taciturn, elderly manservant took his card, whilst Roscoe waited in a charmingly appointed lobby decorated with paintings by Watteau, dainty figurines and period vases. The man came back and took him up in an elevator, leading him to a small panelled room very plainly furnished where Miss Finelander's housekeeper was seated at a neat desk.

She proved to be a dour Scotswoman of forbidding appearance, by name Mrs. Cairn. She showed small respect for the official status of her visitor, bidding him, sternly, to take a seat and fixing him with a look more like that of a prison wardress than anything else.

"What can I do for you, sir?"

Roscoe felt sure that she could, or would, do as little as possible.

"I am sorry to trouble you, ma'am, but in the absence of Miss Finelander, I wonder if you could give me any information about the *John P. Faraway,* which lies off Welfare Island, as you know. Does Miss Finelander ever entertain on board, for instance?"

"Entertain on board!" the lady echoed contemptuously. "Who would she be entertaining? Dockers?"

Roscoe became diplomatic. Possibly, this woman didn't know of the recent police visit to the hulk.

"No." He smiled genially. "I mean she might have had it fitted up for river parties."

"Miss Finelander bought the vessel, as you seem to be aware, with the idea of equipping it as a sea-going yacht. She has never done so."

"Oh, I see. As a keen yachtsman, I thought of doing just that, myself. These pilot craft are fine seaboats, you know."

"They may be, sir. The vessel is not for sale."

"Oh, well, that settles it. Of course, I might consult Miss Finelander. If she has no use for the craft, perhaps—"

Mrs. Cairn stood up.

"You will be wasting your time, sir."

Drake Roscoe accepted his dismissal, as Mrs. Cairn pressed a bell. At the door, he turned, still smiling genially.

"Have you been on board recently, Mrs. Cairn?"

"I have never been on board, sir. I am Miss Finelander's housekeeper, and she understands my duties."

As the elderly manservant reappeared, Roscoe bowed and went out, followed by the baneful stare of Mrs. Cairn. But, driving back to his hotel, he reflected silently: "We find ourselves in very deep water. That woman knows something...."

II

He was told at the desk as he went in, that Tony McKeigh had inquired for him again. But when he called up McKeigh's number there was no reply. This was due to the fact that Tony, at this time, was exploring the numerous public rooms of the hotel, hoping for a glimpse of a girl with blue eyes and distractingly wonderful hair which seemed to vary between chestnut and mahogany as changing light touched it.

Roscoe found a memo from the chief house detective on his desk. It reported that the guest who had occupied the apartment directly above his own, and who had left, hurriedly, on the night before, had proved to be untraceable. He had registered as Peter Delmont, of Valparaiso, and his reservation had been made ahead of his arrival. He had left no forwarding address.

The assignment to this intricate case, taken over at short notice, was one, as Roscoe realized, that called for a resident staff. He must set one up without delay, for this job was going to take time.

He was up against dangerously clever people, who had influential backing. His own apartment should never be empty, now that he had been identified by the enemy. After that revealing interview with Mrs. Cairn he began to wonder if he could trust anybody, even the hotel management.

This had been a very tiring day, and there was much yet to be done. Drake Roscoe helped himself to a generous highball, and sinking into a comfortable armchair, took a cigar from a newly opened box and lighted it, giving a sigh of contentment.

He might justifiably relax for half an hour.

He relaxed so completely that, apart from an uncertain memory of dropping his whisky glass on the floor, he remembered no more, until...

There was someone else in the room!

His head was spinning. A purple haze hung before his eyes. He closed them for a moment, then opened them again. The haze seemed to be dispersing.

But *she* was still there!

A woman lolled indolently on the divan. Although, to Drake Roscoe, the room felt uncomfortably warm, she was wrapped in a

65

mink cloak. She had dropped the fur slightly, so that one bare shoulder and arm were free, to enable her to handle the cigarette which she was smoking. She wore a brightly coloured scarf over her hair, and her eyes, half closed and veiled by insolently long lashes, were fixed upon him—smilingly.

"No—you are not dreaming, Major Roscoe. It's a pity, isn't it? But I am really here."

There was only one voice in the world which held that haunting music—like the magic of harp notes—the voice he had heard over the telephone in William Obershaw's study!

"Yes," the caressing tones went on, "I believe you call me Sumuru. It isn't my name, of course, but it doesn't matter."

Roscoe determined on swift action. He wouldn't waste time bandying words with this lovely, impudent criminal. He would spring, seize her, and by God! once he had her, he'd hold her!

She might be armed; probably was. The attack must be sudden. He would lean forward, watching her, as if still uncertain if he were awake or asleep. He tried to do so. He tried again... tried a third time.

Not a muscle responded! His whole body was inert. Only his brain functioned. And then, a ghastly thought struck his heart cold....

Rigor Kubus!

Sumuru raised her cigarette to her lips.

"Your alarm is unnecessary, Major—or have you dropped the Major? It is not *rigor Kubus*. Believe me, I have no desire to kill you. The world needs such men as you. My mission in life is to preserve what is worthy. I destroy only the ugliness which is defacing all that is worth while. There are those live to-day who toil to deface all beauty—to gnaw it to pieces, morsel by morsel. I call them the sewer rats. These, I endeavour to destroy. Why don't you talk to me? Do you find me unattractive?"

"You female fiend—"

"Isn't there a word fiendess? Every word should have its feminine. The feminine is so important. You see? Your voice is unimpaired. I could have heard you over a full gale."

"By some cunning trick you have drugged me!"

"Cunning trick?" She laughed, and her trilling laughter was bell-like. "It requires little cunning to send someone into your apartment (I obtained a duplicate key to-day) and to insert a speck

66

of powder in all the cigars on the top layer. I must take the others with me, by the way. It is an improved preparation of the drug called in Southern India, *ahbowanee*. It will do you no harm, once the inertia has worn off."

"I am deeply grateful!"

"You sound grateful! Yet, you should be. I have gone to all this trouble just to obtain a private interview with you. There are many men, Mr. Roscoe, who would risk much for the privilege of such a secret visit. I have succeeded in converting to my philosophy—which is simply the philosophy of sanity—some of the world's finest intellects. It is always a sorrow to me when a clever man remains blind to the truth of beauty—which is what God meant all men to strive for."

Drake Roscoe made a choking sound.

"You speak of God! *You!*"

"Yes—I. Many times in your wars at sea, your 'gallant' officers have sunk enemy ships. In those ships were fellow creatures who had never harmed them nor anyone else, who were worthy of life. They loved life, they loved their homes—which, by those gallant hands, they were never to see again."

She stood up, holding the mink cloak about her like a robe.

"I have destroyed life, too. But rarely, in all I have done, has an innocent man or woman died at my hands. I strike down evil. I destroy ugliness. I would not soil my soul with the blood-baths you call honourable warfare. And so, yes—I speak of God."

Roscoe tried to find adequate words. Sumuru, smiling disdainfully, dropped back on the divan. Was there some grain of reason in this woman's angle on life? Her reference to the wholesale destruction of sea warfare had touched him on a sensitive spot. More than once, studying dispatches of the sinking of an enemy ship, he had felt sick at heart.

Or was it all due to her insidious sex appeal? Would he have been so disposed to consider, seriously, all this nonsense if the speaker had been a man?

"No, Mr. Roscoe." Sumuru's lovely voice was low-pitched. "Man rejects man, because men are fighting animals. This is one reason why women should unite, and rule."

She had answered an unspoken thought!

"Was I thinking aloud?"

"I understood you to inquire if my power over men is mere sex appeal."

He tried to shut his eyes, so that he didn't see the beautiful witch who smiled at him alluringly. His lids refused to close!

"Yes, you must keep your eyes open," she said softly. "It is a mysterious drug, this *ahbowanee*. It checks all the muscular functions except those of articulation. But am I so objectionable to look upon?"

She crossed her slim legs, and mocked him under lowered lashes. A picture flashed through his mind, the picture of Celie Artz, rigid, clutching a bed-post.

"Your method of dealing with people who interfere with you must be pleasing to heaven!" He spoke bitterly, hopelessly.

"You are thinking of Sister Celeste? You knew her as Celie Artz. She was a member of the Order. She gave us a child, a boy beautiful as Antinous. He is studying in my Egyptian College. His father was one of your greatest writers—although none of your writers are really great. She became an outside worker—and then a renegade. It was unaccountable, when one considers the type of creature who led her to betray her vows. I had to make an example."

"You certainly succeeded!"

"Nothing and no one must be permitted to interrupt my mission—which is to purge the world of ugliness, to destroy the rule of brute force. There are men alive to-day who burrow in darkness to bring down in ashes what little remains to us of culture, of beauty. These creatures are the sewer rats. Hitler was such a creature."

Sumuru seemed to be inspired, possessed of the spirit of a Cumcean oracle. Her voice added immense authority to her strange words. Roscoe found himself forced to listen in silence, in wrapt silence.

"He despite the most sensational fiasco in human history, has passed on a dream to men less than himself, and to some greater. They see that the power which built the Pyramid of Gizeh was nothing more mysterious than mass labour; that a solo-voice supported by a chorus a million strong can shatter thrones."

She closed her eyes, speaking almost as if in a trance.

"They see that such a force, used in reverse, as sheer inertia, can stifle the heart's blood of a whole nation. At one man's command, 'Cease!' a hundred ships may lie idle at their moorings, a hundred thousand mills be still, the lights of a city go out. A good dream, in the eyes of lesser men.... But such men must be silenced! They are ugly."

Sumuru shuddered, raised her long lashes and stared vaguely at Drake Roscoe. In the next moment she was smiling, the same tantalizing smile.

"Have I been talking unendurable nonsense, Mr. Roscoe? Forgive me if I bored you. As a man, you will find it hard to believe that there can be no harmony in the world until such men, the great and the lesser, are removed from it."

She replaced her black cigarette holder between her lips and recrossed her slender ankles.

Roscoe's gaze became fixed upon those patrician ankles. He could not be sure that Sumuru wore stockings, but, just discernible on her left ankle, he detected a faint outline.

"Are you admiring my justly celebrated legs, or looking for the linked serpent?" She raised her foot, shod in a dainty black shoe, and pointed the toe, like a ballet dancer. "You can see the mark clearly, now. Shall I restore your normal muscular activity so that you can come and examine it more closely?"

A wave of hot embarrassment swept over Drake Roscoe. Mark Donovan had warned him. As he knew, now, and despised himself, his warning had not exaggerated the danger. This woman could seduce a saint!

"I have not tried to arouse your desire, Mr. Roscoe. If I thought you sufficiently important, I might offer myself as a reward. But I would rather appeal to what is higher in you than to that animal appetite which you share with other men. I was curious to meet you, that's all. I like to know the types with whom I have to deal."

"You have much to learn, yet, about *my* type!"

Sumuru extinguished her cigarette in an ash-tray, stood up and carried it out. She returned, having emptied and cleaned the tray. Smiling at Roscoe as she passed close to his chair, she took several cigars from the box and slipped them into a pocket in the lining of her cloak, replacing them with others which she had brought.

He watched her, in silence. He was aware of a faint and quite unusual perfume. What was it?

"*Spikenard,* Mr. Roscoe," she explained, as though he had spoken. "Only one living person knows the secret of its preparation. I must go, as I have an urgent appointment—or do you call it a date in your barbarous *patois?* If you succeed in really troubling me, I may come and see you again. If you merely make yourself a nuisance, I shall send someone else."

She smiled provocatively, draped the mink cloak about her graceful figure and went out into the lobby. He heard the outer door close quietly.

CHAPTER EIGHT

I

Tony McKeigh badly needed to talk to somebody. He was by no means certain of his own sanity. An impression, already fading, of vague perfume in his living-room alone remained to suggest that what he thought had happened had really happened.

His empty pipe, lying beside his pouch on the desk, contradicted his belief that he had been smoking at the moment when oblivion had come. And if that memory had no basis in fact why trust those others—his meeting with Viola, their conversation, her return here to his apartment, her kisses?

Quite certainly, he hadn't floated high up in space, moored to earth only by a slender silk cord, and seen his own body lying far below. His idea that the Duchesse de Severac had been in the room could be explained by his glimpse of that exotically beautiful woman earlier in the day.

Therefore, he must have been the victim of some form of hallucination. There must be something wrong with his brain!

Once again, he tried to call Drake Roscoe. The same result: Mr. Drake Roscoe didn't answer. Something had to be done. It was quite easy to believe that Roscoe had been in and out of his hotel all day, that he had always just missed him. He decided to go along and check this.

He showed his card at the desk, and was told that Roscoe had gone out in the morning but had come in early in the evening, and so far as anybody knew hadn't gone out again.

A sense of apprehension, baseless as he told himself and due to his own high-strung condition, overpowered Tony McKeigh. He seemed to see again, vividly, those petrified bodies. Drake Roscoe was pitted against a group that commanded strange powers, counted human life lightly expendable. He asked the clerk to call Roscoe's apartment.

To his intense relief, the clerk turned and said:

"Mr. Drake Roscoe says to go right up."

Tony McKeigh was shot up by express elevator, to the lofty floor on which Roscoe lived. He walked along and pressed the button.

Drake Roscoe opened the door. His strained expression immediately struck Tony.

"Come in, Mac. Glad to see you."

As Tony went in and Roscoe closed the door:

"Anything wrong, old scout?" Tony asked. "You're moving sort of stiffly."

"Am I?" Roscoe forced a grin. "Sit down. Help yourself. I've just opened another bottle."

"Why stress this bibulous fact?"

"I have reasons."

As Tony McKeigh sat down in an armchair, helped himself to a drink and began to fill his pipe, Drake Roscoe paced up and down, that strange, anxious expression on his face. He swung his arms vigorously and frequently opened and shut his eyes. Pausing suddenly:

"Has it ever occurred to you, Mac," he asked sharply, "that a man—any man—might go suddenly mad?"

Tony laid his half-filled pipe on the table. He had been wondering how to begin the strange and horrifying story of his lapse, and now, here was the very opening!

"It occurred to me to-night, Roscoe!"

"I can't imagine why. Did you ask yourself if some forms of supposed madness may be induced by outside influence—drugs and a kind of hypnotism for instance?"

"No. But the theory has points."

"*Some* theory has to be found. Because to-night I have been made the victim of a singular hallucination!"

"*You* have!"

"I thought, as I sat in that chair where you're sitting now, that I dropped my glass on the floor, lost consciousness, and then revived to find a woman seated on the divan. It was Sumuru! She talked to me, taunted me, and then went out. I couldn't stir a muscle of my body. She said this was due to a drug in my cigar. After she had gone, my phone rang several times. I couldn't move, couldn't reach it. I shouted but nobody answered. Five minutes ago this frightful paralysis left me, quite suddenly, just as you called up from the lobby.

Tony McKeigh, his eyes fixed on the Major, had been rising by inches from his chair, and now:

"Roscoe!" he shouted, "you've saved my sanity! And I think I can save yours!"

"What on earth d'you mean?"

"Tell me—there was no evidence, after this hallucination, or what have you, to prove that it had been real?"

"Not a thing! My empty glass stood beside me. There was no trace of the cigar I thought I had been smoking. The number of cigars in the new box was correct."

"You are sure—now think hard—there was *no perfume* in the room?"

"You're right! you're right! There was, and I could detect it for some time afterwards." He faced Tony McKeigh. "What *do you* know about it?"

Tony dropped back in the armchair and went on filling his pipe. He was torn between wild elation and black depression; for if he had, truly, held Viola in his arms, she had come to trap him.

"Listen!" he said. "I have something to tell you..."

II

As Tony McKeigh's story was told, Drake Roscoe paced the room with a faster and faster stride. At the end:

"Mac!" he snapped. "We can't both have been dreaming, and we're not both mad. But it seems we're both in danger from a gang employing a routine that's unique in my experience. Where *you* come into the picture I don't know. We'll have to find out. There's just one point about your experience, though, which may conceal a clue. So tell me this: you say you thought you saw the Duchesse de Severac bending over your body. Why the Duchesse de Severac? Do you know her?"

No. I only saw her once in my life. She was coming into this hotel and I overheard somebody say, 'That's the Duchesse de Severac, the best-dressed woman in Paris.'"

Roscoe kept on walking.

"Into *this* hotel! When?"

"This afternoon."

"What does she look like?"

"She's a stunner. And—gad! I've got it! I know, now, why I imagined I saw her in my room! It was the *perfume*! Tonight, when I woke up, and noticed traces of a peculiar perfume, I tried to remember where I had come across it before. I remember now. It was when the Duchesse de Severac passed me by!"

"Apart from being a stunner, what type is the lady? Dark? fair?"

Tony McKeigh rubbed his chin reflectively.

"More than a bit difficult to say. She has what I've seen described as a radiant complexion, which may be due to a good make-up, and she carries herself like an empress. She was wearing a long mink cloak—"

"So was Sumuru—and so do many women around here. But what about her eyes?"

"I hadn't a chance to notice."

Roscoe pulled up and stared at Tony McKeigh.

"Maybe one day I'll meet somebody who can describe Sumuru to me! Then I may know when people are talking about her."

"Describe her yourself, dear boy. You say she called on you."

Roscoe's expression changed. Then, the old smile broke through.

"A hit, Mac! I couldn't describe her if they made me President! There's some magic about this woman."

"You're not, by any chance, toying with the bright thought that Sumuru is the Duchesse de Severac?"

Roscoe faced him grimly.

"Why not? She has been married (so it's believed) to a Japanese marquis, to a British peer, and to a Swedish baron. Why not to a French duke? I'll check on the Duchesse, right now!"

He grabbed the phone and asked for a downtown number. When he got it:

"Drake Roscoe here," he said rapidly. "Get me an outline on the Duchesse de Severac. Facts to date. Call back. Make it snappy. Urgent!"

He hung up and began to walk about again.

"The activities of Sumuru, during her stay in London, simply beggar belief, Mac. She practically had diplomatic immunity, for one thing. They discovered that the wife of a foreign ambassador was one of the Order! Oh, the woman's a sorceress. I got first-hand information, this morning, from Mark Donovan, that staggered me."

"What! is Mark in town?"

"No. He lives out in Connecticut. He has a lovely wife and a charming little daughter."

"Good for Mark. Such a shy chap. I can't imagine how he ever whipped up enough woof-woof to tackle a pretty girl."

Drake Roscoe grinned.

"Lack of woof-woof isn't one of your failings, is it? Never was, if I remember. Hullo! There's the phone."

He crossed, picked up the receiver, said, "Yes," and then listened. Tony McKeigh, watching him, saw a series of highly curious expressions making way for one another on the weathered face. When Roscoe hung up, he turned, and the last expression was stern.

"Mac—the Duchesse has been staying as guest of Miss Rhoda Finelander at the Finelander home in Greenwich—"

"Conveying what?"

"Miss Rhoda Finelander was the purchaser of the *John P. Faraway,* which we visited recently! Wait! There's more to come. The Duchesse left Greenwich and arrived in Manhattan yesterday. She occupied a suite on this floor! *You* have seen her in the flesh. I *think* I have seen Sumuru. We agree that they use the same perfume—"

"But, Roscoe! Is there anything on the Duchesse? I mean—"

"You mean, who *is* she? Well, I'll tell you. She's the *widow* of the old Due de Severac, who died six months back and left several million francs behind him! There's no information available as to what or who she was before her marriage two years ago."

Drake Roscoe snatched up the phone.

"Kindly put me through to the Duchesse de Severac's suite," he instructed crisply.

There was a short interval. Tony McKeigh heard the muted voice of the clerk downstairs. Roscoe hung up. He didn't look round for a moment.

"The Duchesse," he said quietly, "is returning to Europe in the *Ile de France,* sailing to-night. She has already gone on board—"

"She's going to slip through your fingers!"

Drake Roscoe glanced at his watch.

"She isn't! I may have to let her go—but not until I've *seen* her! I'll have the ship held. Stand by for a whirlwind drive to the French Line dock—"

III

All the gangways but one had been cleared when Drake Roscoe and Tony McKeigh came on to the floodlighted dock. They ran up. The chief officer met them on deck.

"I had the Captain's orders, sir," he told Roscoe, "that we were not to sail until we had word from you. As it happens—" he consulted his watch— "we have five minutes in hand. If you could possibly—"

"I'll do my best," Roscoe broke in crisply. "I won't hold your sailing if it can be avoided. Will you please send word to the Duchesse de Severac that Mr. Drake Roscoe wishes to see her."

The ship's officer saluted and hurried off.

Few passengers were in sight on deck. Visitors had gone ashore half an hour earlier. Parties were over. Everybody would be busy preparing to turn in.

"I admit I feel more than a trifle abashed," Tony confided to Roscoe. "After all, if your somewhat fantastic theories prove to be hokum, we shall have a well-below-zero reception—"

"Trust to your *nose!* Sumuru told me (if I didn't dream it) that the perfume she used was *spikenard,* that only one living man knew how to prepare it. And don't let her hypnotize you!"

The chief officer returned at a run.

"Be good enough to follow me..."

The Duchesse's suite was on A deck. A dark-eyed lady's maid stood at the door. The chief officer, who had led them, seemed disposed to linger—and Tony McKeigh didn't blame the Frenchman. The maid was one of the most perfect brunettes he had ever seen.

"Gentlemen"—she spoke charming, broken English— "Madame la Duchesse is prepare to retire. If there is something I can do—"

"I'm sorry, ma'm'selle"—Roscoe spoke briskly— "but I must speak to the Duchesse, personally."

"She have had so tiring a day—"

"Dolores!" came an imperious voice, "admit these gentlemen. I will see them."

Drake Roscoe started, glanced at Tony McKeigh. That clear voice reminded him of Ethel Barrymore, but not of Sumuru. It had, too, a pronounced French accent.

"If you please, messieurs."

The dark-eyed maid stood aside, holding the door open.

They walked into a small lobby in which were a number of suitcases, wardrobe trunks and hat-boxes, from there into an elegantly appointed sitting-room. On a Louis Quinze sofa above which hung a reproduction of a Fragonard, the Duchesse de Severac was seated.

She wore a loose-sleeved blue robe with a deep lace collar. A lace cap quite concealed her hair. She sat stiffly upright, surveying her visitors through a raised lorgnette, so that the lace sleeve fell back from one snowy arm. Tony McKeigh inhaled sharply. He had recognized the Duchesse at once.

But there was no trace of perfume in the cabin.

He glanced at Drake Roscoe—and Roscoe's expression defied description.

"Madame"—Roscoe bowed— "it is possible that I intrude—"

"More than possible, m'sieur," the vibrant voice assured him.

His glance devoured the beautiful, disdainful face. He would have been prepared to swear in a court of law that the woman before him was the woman who had visited his apartment earlier that night. So far, then, he had been right. The Duchesse de Severac was Sumuru!

This should lead to developments. But he recognized, also, that he had not one scrap of evidence to prove that she, or anyone else, had been there at that time. Apart from this incredible visit, he had never seen Sumuru. He couldn't possibly arrest a distinguished Frenchwoman on so monstrous a charge because she resembled someone who had come and gone like a mirage!

Yet, it was infuriating to be forced to let her slip away.

"I believe, Madame, that you stayed recently at the Savoy Babylon Hotel?"

"I believe so."

"And I understand that you are a friend of Miss Finelander?"

"I am."

The lorgnette never stirred. The gaze of the Duchesse never wavered. Her deep voice held a note of contemptuous annoyance.

"I had hoped that from her you might have learned some thing about the present whereabouts of Miss Obershaw—"

"Of whom, m'sieur?"

"Miss Sally Obershaw."

"I am unacquainted with the lady. If that is all you came to ask of me I regret that I cannot help you. Dolores! These gentlemen are ready to leave."

They were off the dock and back in the police car before Roscoe spoke again.

"She evidently sees that she has stirred up a hornets' nest," he muttered. "It's humiliating to have to let her go. The change of voice is wonderful, but I could take oath that that's Sumuru. All I can do is to pass the inquiry to the Paris Surete. It's maddening!"

Five minutes later, halted by a red light, they heard the deep note of the whistle as the *Ile de France* was warped out of her berth. Tony McKeigh had become strangely silent. He was trying to pin down a phantom memory. He had concentrated so completely on identifying that peculiar perfume, that some other mark of identification which he had filed away mentally, for future reference, refused to be discovered.

The police driver was speeding on again when revelation came.

McKeigh grasped Roscoe's arm.

"Roscoe! Roscoe! That woman may or may not be Sumuru, but one thing I'm sure about—she isn't the Duchesse de Severac!"

"What on earth do you mean? You told me you recognized her on sight."

"So I did—or thought I did. But I'm beginning to agree with you that we're dealing with witchcraft. I have just remembered something. It's something I happened to notice—and then like a fool forgot—when the Duchesse passed close by me as she went into the Savoy Babylon—"

"Well—what was it?"

"Her ear!"

"Her *ear?*"

"That woman on the *Ile de France* is uncannily like the Duchesse de Severac—except in that one respect. The real Duchesse has ears like a faun—no lobes!"

IV

Our Lady was refreshing herself in her swimming-pool. She dived like a mermaid and swam like one. Her power to remain for a long time under water was phenomenal. It was necessary for the enjoyment of the sport in which she was indulging.

The swimming-pool (one day to become an object of wonder to those who had not seen it before) probably had no duplicate anywhere in the world. The bottom and sides appeared to be made of crystal, or of some thick, crystal-clear glass. Below the crystal bottom of the pool, and behind the crystal sides and ends, was a much larger pool, so that the bath itself might be said to hang suspended in it.

Here were coral grottoes and all sorts of marine plants, and swimming about in this miniature Caribbean, numbers of gaily coloured tropical fish of grotesque but charming shapes, among them a grey and ominous barracuda some four feet long. From narrow ledges surrounding rose the sides of a crystal roof which covered with its arch the entire pool. Behind this, dwarf palms rose gracefully from flowering shrubs and banks of flowers. The fanlike leaves of the palms stretched across the arch as if to greet each other.

The pool was invisibly lighted from above to reproduce tropical sunshine.

Her hair hidden under a rubber cap, Sumuru might have been mistaken for Derceto, the fish goddess, or for a water-nymph. Her effortless ease was a poem of movement, her white limbs gleaming in the clear water as she glided here and there.

At the head of a flight of movable steps which gave access to the pool, a negro girl stood, motionless, holding a bathrobe of white fleece. She resembled an ebony statue of African beauty. Only her gleeful smile, displaying glittering teeth, disturbed the illusion.

Sumuru's sport was peculiar.

She would dive into the pool, and swim along the crystal bottom. Instantly, the brilliant fish, purple, green, scarlet, would disperse. But, always, the barracuda attacked. Dashing his vicious snout against the glass which separated him from his prey, he would snap at a white arm, a tempting ankle, only to retire foiled, baffled—and then attack again.

Sumuru would tempt and taunt the killer fish as long as she could remain underwater; then, coming to the top, breathless, she would laugh delightedly, the beautiful negress joining in her glee....

"Satan thought he had me that time, Bella!"

"I'd be sorry for you, Madonna, if the glass broke."

At last, coming up breathless from the depths of the pool, Sumuru received a message from the negress.

"Caspar reports that Philo is back, Madonna."

Madonna shook her head to clear water from her long lashes and swam to the foot of the steps. She ran up. The ivory statue stood beside the ebony. Bella wrapped Sumuru in the fleece robe and followed her up three glass steps which led out of the pool.

Only a few minutes had passed when Caspar noiselessly opened a door in the panelled wall of the room with a blue canopy and crossed, smiling his eternal smile, to where Sumuru lay stretched luxuriously on a mound of cushions piled on the fur rugs beside the marble fishpond. She was wrapped in a cloak of snow mink, so that only her face and one small foot, hardly hidden by a gilt Roman sandal, were visible.

Caspar performed his customary *salaam.*

"Madonna, Philo is waiting."

"Send him to me."

Caspar retired, his red slippers whispering on the tiles and becoming silent when he stepped on the mink rugs. As he went through the doorway:

"Our Lady wants Philo," he called.

"Philo!" came from beyond.

"Philo ..."

Our Lady sipped thick Turkish coffee from a small cup which she took from an Arab table beside her.

A man came in who wore a chauffeur's dark grey uniform. Although of no more than medium height, he had a tremendous shoulder span, and his depth of chest and length of arms suggested great strength. Thick black hair grew low on his narrow forehead, but his otherwise brutal appearance was redeemed by the quick intelligence in his eyes. His tread was strangely silent.

He crossed and stood beside Sumuru, in an attitude of complete deference.

"Sit there, Philo, on the edge of the pond. It wearies me to look up so far."

"Yes, My Lady."

Philo sat down, his eyes fixed on the lovely face in a look of doglike devotion. He had a deep voice and spoke with a marked accent.

"You waited until the ship sailed, I am told."

"I did, My Lady."

"You saw Sister Hyacinthe, Sister Sarah, Sister Dolores safely to their suite?"

"Yes, My Lady."

"After you came ashore, tell me what occurred."

"A police car drove in. Two men ran on to the dock and up the gangway, which had been held for them, I think. A senior ship's officer was waiting to receive them."

"Did you know these men, Philo?"

"I recognized one, My Lady. It was the man known as The Major. Sanchez, who was with me, recognized the other as the Englishman, McKeigh."

Sumuru lighted a cigarette.

"This corresponds with all I have heard. You saw these men come ashore?"

"Yes, My Lady, five minutes later. They drove to the Savoy Babylon. I followed them."

My Lady smiled graciously.

"All goes well. Yet"—her look grew introspective— "I begin to wonder about this man Roscoe, to wonder what aroused his suspicion that we were one and the same."

"You invited this, My Lady!" Philo bravely sustained a glance of those strange eyes. "You play with danger. It is your sport."

Sumuru smiled again, and stretched herself in luxurious ease.

"How insolent you are, Philo. Sometimes, you venture on most unwarrantable liberties." But there was no reproach in the golden voice. "You may go, Philo."

Philo stood up and went out quite silently. A leopard could not have made less noise in crossing the fur-strewn floor.

CHAPTER NINE

I

"THE hardest thing for me to bear," Tony McKeigh told Drake Roscoe, "is being gagged. Here's an inside story on the biggest racket Manhattan has ever known, and I can't release a single par."

"There's this disastrous dock strike," Roscoe suggested, smiling slyly. "It has completely tied up the Port of New York. What about telling 'em to interview Steve Mason, the Labour boss responsible?"

"They sought the same—and drew a blank. Steve Mason seems to imagine his life is in danger. He lies entrenched behind a bodyguard of professional thugs."

Roscoe stared out of the window. A panorama of a large part of the City lay below leading the eye on and on, out to the open sea. Somewhere, perhaps within sight from his window, Sumuru was at work, planning new outrages. He turned, looked at Tony.

"Something else you find hard to bear, Mac. But don't say I didn't warn you. You're always day-dreaming about the girl who told you her name was Viola Stayton. As it's certain she doped your whisky or your tobacco, you have an odd taste in girl friends!"

Tony McKeigh jumped up restlessly.

"The thing gets between me and my work, Roscoe. I find it hard to carry on."

"Well"—Drake Roscoe lighted a cigar— "I guessed as much. You seem to be as deep in this business as I am. Clues have been poked under your nose, and you have made certain contacts. This girl Viola is one. At the moment, you're more valuable to me than you are to the *Telegram.*"

"You mean—I deserve to be fired?" No, They have another man who could carry on in your absence. The job stays open, if you want to go back."

"Who says I've lost my job?"

"Nobody. It adds to your value in the eyes of the London office."

"*What* adds to my value?"

"Being asked for by the Federal authority. The *Telegram* has given you three months' leave to work under me."

Tony McKeigh gasped.

"Do you really mean this, Roscoe? Has the great man in London given me his blessing?"

"I mean it—and he has. He's delighted to know that one of his young men is so hot that the United States government wants to borrow him. So when you have tidied things up in the office, you can put in full time here."

Tony McKeigh saluted and then held out his hand.

"Thanks, Roscoe. It's abduction, because I wasn't consulted. But I like it."

Drake Roscoe smiled his grimmest smile.

"I warn you—it's a murderous job. And I expect hard work from my staff."

"So I found out when I toiled under you before, sir!"

Roscoe crossed to his desk.

"I can now let you see all the Scotland Yard documents. You may spot something I have overlooked. Here are queries which we have to answer: (1) Is Sumuru the Duchesse de Severac? (2) Is the woman now *en route* for France in the *Ile de France* the real Duchesse? (This inquiry passed to Paris Surete.) (3) Has anyone called Viola Stayton disappeared from England? (to be passed to Scotland Yard with your description of the lady). (4) Has Sally Obershaw voluntarily joined this Order or has she been abducted? (5) Where is Sally Obershaw? (6) Is Miss Rhoda Finelander a member? (7) Does she know that Sally spent a week on the *John P. Faraway?* (8) Where is Sumuru's New York base? (9) What is Sumuru's interest in Tony McKeigh?—Any comments?"

"No. I'm staggered. It's a monumental job."

"We don't work alone. Then, there's the Donovans. Claudette Donovan could tell us a lot more, I believe, but she's scared stiff, poor girl. I, for one, don't blame her."

Tony began to fill his pipe. Nearly a week had gone by since that midnight dash to the *Ile de France*. Nothing whatever occurred in the interval to suggest that the hand of Sumuru was at work.

The door-bell buzzed. Tony McKeigh glanced at Roscoe, then went and opened the door. He signed for a radiogram, which he handed to Roscoe.

Drake Roscoe glanced at the message and tossed it back to Tony.

"From Paris. It's in code. You'll find the book in that bureau. Your old job, if I remember?"

"One of 'em. Seeing you didn't run out of ice-water for your whisky was another."

Tony settled himself at the bureau to decode the message. It was brief and to the point. It said:

"Duchesse de Severac interviewed on her way through Paris to Chateau Carron. Stop. Identified by member of family, Vicomte de Severac. Finis."

"As I expected!" Roscoe threw the transcription on his desk. "If you're right—and I don't doubt it—Sumuru will have sent instructions ahead to deal with such a possibility. This case is like trying to trap a will-o'-the-wisp!"

II

Drake Roscoe had hit the mark when he assured Tony McKeigh that Claudette Donovan could tell more about Sumuru than she had so far cared to tell. Roscoe had finished *Tears of Our Lady,* and had learned from that vaguely repellent yet brilliant book that women were designed by their Creator to be, not men's mistresses, but men's masters. So-called "love matches," he learned, produced the most desirable offspring. Therefore, such unions should be encouraged—but only for this purpose.

Children so born, the author stated, must be removed from the harmful influence of "parent love" at an early age. One of the parents might lack that true sense of beauty which alone can produce the proper atmosphere in which a future member of the Order should be brought to maturity.

There were references to an "Egyptian college" and to "The Greek school" (which suggested to Roscoe that such institutions actually existed) where children of members of this unnamed "Order" were trained from infancy in Sumuru's philosophy of life.

He had begun to understand Claudette's despairing cry— "She will try to get my baby...."

There was a certain parallel with Nazi ideals in this stressing of a future race dedicated to one purpose; only the purpose was different: the glorification of Woman, the outlawing of ugliness, the abolition of war.

And at about the time that Roscoe drew McKeigh's attention to nine queries which had to be answered, Mark Donovan, his arm around Claudette, was standing at an open window watching Claudette II playing in the garden. Her nurse, a pretty Irish girl, sat near-by, reading.

85

"Don't you think Claudette, *cherie*, you're making yourself unhappy for no reason?"

Claudette shook her head. There were shadows under her eyes.

"I thought, dear, that when we came here, we should be free of her. But now that she is so near again..."

"I know how you feel about her—and I know you're right. She's the most dangerous woman in the world. I have still to be convinced that she's really human. But after all, baby is hardly ever out of our sight. You don't think"—Mark frowned in his perplexed way— "that Sumuru hates me because of what I wrote about her in England?"

"No, my dear!" Claudette squeezed his arm. "If she had objected, you would never have been allowed to publish it!"

"You think she has all that influence?"

"I *know* she has. There are people in high places, all over the world, who carry out her orders without question. Mark, dear! She's quite above the law. She only respects one law—her own. I haven't wanted to worry you, but"—her gaze wandered to the fluffy-haired little girl setting out a dolls' party on the lawn— "two things have happened since Mr. Drake Roscoe was here."

"What things?" Mark's tone was anxious.

"Neither may mean anything, but everything seems to have a hidden meaning when I know that *she* is about. Detty" (Claudette II so pronounced her name) "has taken to talking about someone she calls 'booful lady.'"

"She means you," Mark told her affectionately. Claudette shook her head again.

"She doesn't, Mark. I have tried. Then I thought it might be a name for one of her dolls. But I was wrong again. I might have forgotten it, but only to-day I took out my mink coat—your extravagant birthday present, darling!—because I thought I had seen a moth in the closet. I had hung the coat on a branch to air the fur just as Anna came back with Detty from their morning walk."

Claudette hesitated. As always, when she was excited, her accent, which Mark adored, had become more marked. He held her close.

"Well—what, *cherie?*"

"She didn't seem to notice *me* at all. As Anna wheeled the pram past the tree, Detty reached out and stroked the fur. She laughed, that little chuckling laugh she has when she's happy, and—"

"Yes, darling?"

"Said 'Booful lady! Booful lady!'" Mark stared aside at Claudette. "It was curious. But why should it frighten you?"

"Because Our Lady never wears any fur but mink."

"Claudette, my dearest, I quite understand. But, truly, you are letting your imagination run away with you. Detty must have seen a picture of someone wearing fur like that. And don't forget she has seen *you* wearing it."

"I know. But she wasn't thinking of me. I'm sure, I'm sure!"

Mark Donovan wrinkled his forehead. "If you mean what I suppose you mean, Claudette, where could Detty have seen this beautiful lady? Could only be when she was out with Anna. I'll talk to Anna."

"No, don't, darling. I have talked with her already. She agrees with you that baby's 'booful lady' is imaginary. But it was from Anna that I heard about the other thing. Anna tells me that there's a queer-looking man who's always appearing in the lane when she goes out with Detty."

Mark laughed, and tightened his clasp of Claudette's slim waist.

"That really *is* imagining things, *cherie*! Anna's quite a good-looking girl. It's some local admirer who's too shy to talk to her."

Claudette nestled her head against his shoulder.

"As you were too shy, once, to talk to *me!* Oh, I wish I could believe that. I'm afraid it isn't true, from what Anna tells me. She says she has only seen this man because she has a feeling of being watched, and has got into a habit of suddenly looking back. He always disappears like a ghost."

"Does he?" Mark squared his jaw. "This afternoon, I'll slip out ahead of Anna—don't tell her—and find out if my fist goes through this ghost!"

III

Our Lady was seated in the high-backed armchair of blackened oak, behind the narrow table littered with papers and lighted by a lamp on an ancient Egyptian pedestal. The rest of the small library remained masked in shadow. She wore a grey suit and a hat which proclaimed its Parisian origin by its mere originality. A platinum mink cape lay on the carpet beside her, beside the cape a pair of pale grey gloves.

She was talking on the phone.

"You clearly understand, Sister Juno? Your unsuitable marriage, although I permitted it, displeased me. You have done something for the Order to make amends—if only financially. You are now engaged on an important service. What you tell me is satisfactory—so far. I shall be personally interested in your further conduct of the matter."

She listened awhile; the expression on her beautiful face mingled perplexity and doubt. But presently:

"You seem to understand," she said, the musical voice soft as distant harps. "For your sake, and for the sake of us all, I trust you do."

When she hung up, she pressed a button. There was no sound, but almost immediately a door opened and Caspar came in, smiling. He *salaamed* deeply.

"You called me, My Lady?"

Sumuru didn't look up. She was studying a page of notes on the table before her.

"Advise Philo to stand by day and night. Notify Silvestre. I may require the plane at short notice."

"Yes, My Lady."

"The last report from Sister Annette is late. See to this. Is Ariosto here?"

"He is, My Lady."

"Send him to me."

Caspar bowed and went out as silently as he had come in. He seemed to fade into the shadows. No sounds from outside penetrated to this room. Nothing disturbed its quiet until Ariosto opened a door and stood before Sumuru.

"You wanted me, Madonna?"

He wore a long, white coat of the kind used by doctors, and seemed to have been called from important work.

"Yes. Am I disturbing you?" Sumuru's voice and manner were cold.

"You have always disturbed me," Ariosto told her, a note of repressed ardour in his speech.

"So you have mentioned before."

"Why did you send Dolores away?"

Then Sumuru looked up. Ariosto challenged those wonderful eyes, but not for long. He glanced aside.

"Does her absence also disturb you?"

"No, Madonna. I only hope she has not displeased you."

"On the contrary, she is highly intelligent, and pleases me in every way. She may be in France for some little time. It is possible, Ariosto, that I shall be leaving this dreary city for a short journey, and shall require you to go with me—"

"Madonna!"

"Yes?"

The fire died out of the man's eyes under that keen scrutiny, and he answered humbly:

"I am always happy to be with you."

"And always the courtier, my friend. You know the nature of the affair upon which we are engaged. Coming so shortly after the trouble with Sister Celeste, it is regrettable. But, all the same, we must act. To date, our plans have worked to perfection. We must complete them."

Ariosto's expression was one of hesitation.

"Sister Juno has never been reliable, Madonna. Your danger in the event of detection, or failure, could be terrible."

Madonna laughed—sweetly rippling laughter like that of a carefree child, or of a wood-nymph when the world was young.

"Danger, my friend? How dull life becomes unless we live it dangerously...."

IV

"You see, Mac," Drake Roscoe was saying, "how wise I was to take you over. I can nearly manage to be in two places at once, but not in three. This blasted dock strike and the disappearance of Steve Mason have piled on too heavy a load."

"Steve Mason?" Tony McKeigh removed his pipe, stared at Roscoe. "No doubt, most excellent chief, you will be kind enough to tell me what possible interest you can have in said squirp?"

Roscoe's expression didn't reflect Tony's facetious humour—largely forced, because he believed he had lost Viola for ever.

"The interest every citizen must have in the fact that the man in question has held up vital supplies for overseas, and also held up vital essentials for home industries."

"Agreed. But your job isn't like the old Pinkerton assignments, is it? I mean, you're not in the strike-breaking business?"

"I am not. In the case of a character like Steve Mason, I almost wish I were! But somebody else *is* interested in the gentleman!"

Tony McKeigh stared.

"On my commonplace, pedestrian intelligence," he declared, "your remarks fail to ping. The man Mason controls the dock workers. He's called 'em all out. And now, he has disappeared. Do you mean somebody has got him?"

Roscoe shook his head, doubtfully.

"I'm not certain. But I *am* certain that he's a marked man. I never gave you a detailed account of what Sumuru said to me. Ever since that interview took place, I have felt so damned ashamed of myself! The woman treats me as a joke. However—she spoke of petty *fuehrers,* of whom Mason is one, who have the power to 'stifle the heart's blood of a whole nation'. (The words are hers.)"

"Good Lord! You think—"

"I don't *think,* Mac. I *know*! Sumuru is not merely a collector of those she considers fit to live, and to give new beauty the world. She is also a destroyer—of those she considers *unfit* to live. She told me that such men must be silenced. She called them 'ugly'."

A sense as of ice-water trickling down his spine attacked Tony McKeigh. He was thinking that he had dared to fall in love with one of Sumuru's chosen women. He was wondering if "Our Lady" considered *him* unfit to live—ugly!

"In short, Roscoe, you mean that you suspect Sumuru of being concerned in the disappearance of this labour boss?"

Roscoe shook his head again, this time emphatically. He was striding up and down the room restlessly.

"Suspect nothing of the kind! I believe he's gone into hiding—taken cover."

"From what?"

Drake Roscoe paused as he passed the desk, took up a card and tossed it to McKeigh.

"From that!"

Bewildered, uneasy, Tony caught the card. It was a piece of near-white material which resembled vellum. The message on it was written in Old English gilt letters. And this was the message:

"You have not resigned your presidency of the union, as you were instructed to do. You will receive one more warning. La Femme."

He stared at the card, blankly. It looked, at first glance, like an invitation to a wedding. Then he read the message again, and laid the card on the desk.

"Crisp and to the point. I don't believe it would frighten even me."

Drake Roscoe regarded him grimly.

"It frightened Steve Mason. You see, he's had others. And nobody has been able to find out where they come from. The body-guard of professional thugs to which you referred recently deserted *en bloc,* I understand, two days ago. I could bet a thousand dollars to a peanut that 'La Femme' is Sumuru!"

"I deplore your gambling instincts, Roscoe. But you may be right. You mean that this subtle persecution has broken the nerve of Steve Mason? Funny thing, how these tough guys have always a weak spot."

"His nerve was broken so badly that he appealed to the Police Department! They have been covering him ever since I heard about it, and drew my own conclusions. The position is this: Mark Donovan called me early this morning. I'm worried about the state of affairs up there in Wilton—"

"Worried about Mark? Where does *he* come in?"

"I don't think he does, poor devil. But his wife and his child do. Tell you later. I'm committed to keep an eye on that household, Mac. So I can't leave until certain arrangements have been carried out. Therefore, *you* must go."

"Go? Go where?"

"Reliable reports state that Steve Mason left, secretly, for the South last night. He's been checked up. He has a girl friend (married) in Fort Lauderdale, Florida. That's where he's gone. She's not the only one, I understand, but she's the only one he can trust. I want you on the spot, and I'll tell you what you have to find out—you'll be there, of course, as a newspaper man."

CHAPTER TEN

I

Tony McKeigh might have enjoyed his swift transition from New York to Florida, if every hour's flight hadn't taken him further away from any chance of seeing Viola again.

He tried to become resigned to his fate. He had fallen in love for the first time in his carefree life, and he would have to forget it. Such things had happened to other men, thousands of them. They had managed to live it down, and so must he. He forced himself to think of something else.

The facts about Mark Donovan were mysterious and vaguely horrifying. Drake Roscoe clearly believed that Sumuru had designs on the little girl. Tony didn't know what precautions Roscoe had taken, but he knew that he planned to pay the Donovans another visit.

Fixed up in an unobtrusive hotel, where a reservation had been made for him, McKeigh established contacts, arranged by Roscoe, which would enable him to make the acquaintance of Mrs. Charles Madderley—reputed to be Steve Mason's mistress. (In fact, the only person in Lauderdale who didn't seem to know this would appear to be Charles Madderley.)

He then reported back to Drake Roscoe.

"Any rumour that Steve Mason is in town?" Roscoe asked.

"Not a thing, so far. But the affair is common property around here. Is husband-Charles complaisant or blind?"

"Don't know anything about it, Mac. That's your pidgin."

"There's a party at the Madderley home to-morrow night. I'm going."

"H'm! a party? That doesn't seem to add up. Standby, all the same. My information can't be wrong."

"Any developments at your end?" Only one. William Obershaw has had another letter from Sally! She asks him and her mother to forgive her for all the anxiety she has caused them and says she can explain when she sees them."

"Good Lord! Cool damsel. Where did this letter come from?"

"From Chateau Carron in the Rhone Valley—the country home of the Duc de Severac! Mac! I made a fool of myself that night aboard the *Ile de France*—again! I never troubled to ask how many were in the Duchesse's party! I learn from the company that she had a secretary with her. That 'secretary' was Sally Obershaw!"

II

"A peaceful world is an idle dream. When the insects whose catacombs—we call them coral—on which we stand now, were alive and working, the world was at war. Many thousands of years have passed. But the world is still at war."

"Trite, but true," Tony McKeigh commented.

Mrs. Madderley's party was in full swing. He had stepped out for a breath of cool night air and had found this attractive fellow-guest similarly employed. He didn't recall having seen her before.

His glance swept over her. She looked taller than, in fact, she was. Her slenderness appeared reedlike, graceful and pliant without angularity. A scarf tied over her hair disguised its true shade—and she wore tinted sunglasses. As the breeze was quite light he wondered if she might be a film actress—for studio lights make the eyes very sensitive. But her shoulders gleamed like ivory in the moonlight. No trace of sun-tan there. As if conscious of his scrutiny, she replaced a stole of snow mink which had slipped slightly.

The radio had begun to play again. Sounds of laughter reached their ears from the house.

"Are you going back to dance?" she asked.

"No." He shook his head. "I'm not properly dressed—and I didn't come to dance."

"Why did you come—to meet someone?"

"Not exactly."

"Perhaps you are sorry you came?"

Her voice was exquisite, possessing most haunting cadences.

"On the contrary. I'm glad. But perhaps *you* want to dance?"

She laughed softly.

"If I were to tell you how long it is since I did, I doubt if you would believe me."

"Why?"

"Reporters are so sceptical."

"What makes you think I'm a reporter?"

"You have the hungry look of a news-hound baulked of an inky bone."

He laughed. His suspicions were confirmed. That Steve Mason had gone to earth in this small town, Drake Roscoe was almost certain. Very well. Tony had learned a lot about Steve's way of life. His acquaintance was one of Mason's show-pieces. He had been spotted, and she had been detailed to put him off the scent! Clever work, but wasted.

That musical voice breathed softly:

"No—I am not out of Mr. Mason's aviary."

For one magnetic moment the implication of those words missed him. Then he stopped, stared at her. He was really startled. He saw a profile like that of an El Greco virgin, and forced himself to speak.

"Who suggested that you were?"

"You. It was crude. His women are so vulgar."

"I never spoke."

"How queer," she murmured.

They had been pacing slowly along palm-bordered streets and had come to one which led to the ocean. It showed empty from end to end. Strains of the radio had faded long since, grown inaudible. She had not halted when he did, but had merely slackened her pace. He walked on again beside her.

At a point where a waterway gleamed bladelike between two bungalows, and a clump of royal palms framed a crescent moon, he found himself spiritually transported to Ismailia in Egypt, where he had been stationed for a time. There were royal palms everywhere. He knew he must always associate this woman with royal palms. Then, out from the next home—a miniature hacienda—a remark in ripe Pennsylvanian beetled through the night to remind him that he was in Florida, in the real estate belt.

A small plane with a curiously noiseless engine circled over-head, a man-made night-hawk. Flowers, like flames, burned in the hedges. The air, when the breeze dropped, was hot and humid. Suddenly, his companion laughed her soft, trilling laugh.

"You must really get out of the habit of thinking aloud," she said. "I assure you I have no such motives. I am not interested in local scandal, and I'm not in the employ of the F.B.I."

He had been considering all these possibilities—silently! Now, he was becoming fascinated, puzzled—and resentful. He was about to speak, when:

"Why are you hunting Steve Mason?" she asked, casually.

"I wanted to find out why he went into hiding." (Difficult to fence with this woman!)

"He has many enemies."

"But plenty of protection."

"The members of his bodyguard recently disappeared. Did you know that?"

"It was rumoured, but not confirmed."

"Surely such a thing was enough to frighten even a big labour boss?"

"But, as you're not a friend of said boss, where, might I ask, did you pick up this news item?"

"I have an acquaintance in a well-known detective agency. Steve Mason retained their services some time ago."

"H'm! Have they formed any theory?"

"Nothing definite. But they thought it pointed to a pending attack on his life. Perhaps you have a theory of your own?"

He shook his head. "The mantle of the lamented Sherlock H. hasn't fallen upon me, I fear."

"Ah!" It was a soft, an appealing sigh. "One power alone can save the world from the greed, the lust, and the stupidity of the men who rule it."

"What power is that?"

"The power of genius. Genius alone can hope to build a new world on the wreckage of the old one." She flashed him a swift smile, then turned her head aside. "We have fallen far below Plato's ideal with our so-called civilization. So far below that only drastic measures can save mankind from total destruction. Labour strikes, international disorders, even world wars, are not brought about by the masses who suffer by them, who die in their millions because of them. Each of these catastrophes is brought about by a small group of warped ugly men. Sometimes, by one man alone—a man such as Steve Mason."

McKeigh remained silent. He was wondering.

"Great armies cannot avert war. It is necessary only to deal with those who dream of employing them; those who devise space-rockets to carry atomic warheads, lethal gas to destroy whole populations, plans to seize lands which don't belong to them, or strikes to paralyse honest industry—"

McKeigh found his voice. "What would you do about it—murder these lads?"

"Murder them?" She flashed him another of her dazzling smiles. "Really, Mr. McKeigh!"

He was now so tensed up, so well accustomed to this woman's uncanny power to hear unspoken thoughts, that her use of his name passed almost unnoticed.

"When an officer of the Army, or the Navy, orders fire to be concentrated on a point held by the enemy, and all the defenders are killed, do you say that he has murdered them? No—I should simply propose to remove the leprous source of such—shall we say, haemorrhages?—before it can spread and corrupt whole nations. Such warfare would be intensive—a war to end war."

McKeigh pulled up short. This strange, alluring woman was beginning to frighten him. He experienced a chilly sensation in the spine. But all he managed to say was, "Shall we turn back?"

They stood at the brink of the highway. Below, the sea glittered, corrugated by tidal ripples. She faced him now for a moment, and laughed—that bell-like caressing music.

"Turning back is sometimes so difficult," she murmured.

And something in her voice—a memory of a perfect profile glimpsed outside the Savoy Babylon and of words spoken by Drake Roscoe—combined to form a frightful conviction.

He was talking to *Sumuru*—

Came a sudden urgent rush of soft-shod feet, pad-like, as of a baboon. McKeigh twisted about in a flash—but still too late.

He divined, rather than saw, a black-clad figure looming over him.

He saw, he heard, no more....

III

Several hours earlier, a curious incident had occurred in faraway Connecticut.

Mark Donovan always experienced a sense of relief when Claudette II was safe in bed for the night. The growing alarm of her nurse, Anna, which the girl was unable to hide, had had its effect on Claudette's overstrained nerves. Twice again, Anna swore to having seen "the ghost" shadowing her when she had been out with Detty.

Claudette was becoming desperately anxious.

"I think we should report it to the police," she told Mark.

He gave her a reassuring grin.

"Drake Roscoe knows all the facts, *cherie.* I called him some time back and told him about this mysterious prowler. I have never caught a glimpse of him, myself, but if I do, he'll prowl no more!"

"Mark!" Claudette's pretty accent became pronounced in her agitation. "Take care! If it is one of *her* men, he will be very dangerous."

On this particular occasion, Claudette was upstairs telling her small daughter a goodnight story. Detty had developed a habit of demanding that the "booful lady" should be a character in such stories, but Claudette had quite failed to learn from the child what the beautiful lady should look like.

Anna had retired to her own quarters. The coloured help had gone.

Mark slipped out quietly through the kitchen, and immediately took cover in a clump of rhododendrons just outside the door. It was a cloudy evening and very still. He crept cautiously along, around an angle of the house, and paused just under the window of the nursery. He could see light shining out over his head. It touched the trunks of a clump of silver birches which grew on the edge of the lawn, transforming them to phantoms.

Claudette's clear voice reached him:

"The poor little girl, all alone with her friend the white rabbit knew she was lost in the wood. When—what do you think she saw coming through the trees?"

"Booful lady!" came Detty's eager response.

Mark quietly passed along. Although he pretended to treat it lightly, this queer obsession of the child worried him as much as it worried Claudette. Anna assured him that they had never met such a person during their regular daily outings that she was completely at a loss to account for the idea.

Making his way by a detour, under cover, to the other side of the grass, Mark stood listening for any sound which might betray the presence of a hidden watcher. He had to suppose that "the ghost's" attention would be focused on Detty.

Not a sound came from the thicket. He turned and looked up at the lighted window. It was protected by an iron grille. In any event, he felt sure that direct attack was not characteristic of Sumuru. More subtle methods were to be feared.

He resumed his silent patrol, drawing close to the house again.

He saw a light in Anna's room on the ground floor, and the window was partly open. A low hedge bordered the path before the window, and from where he stood, hidden in shrubbery, he thought, at first glance, that it seemed more dense at one point, but concluded that this was due to some effect of shadow.

Faintly, the nurse's voice became audible. She must be talking on the phone.

Then—the patch of dense shadow moved slightly!

Someone was crouching under the window.

Mark's hand slid to his hip pocket. He had not admitted the fact to Claudette, but her warning about Sumuru's men being dangerous, added to his own experience, suggested taking no chances.

In three bounds he crossed the space between and jabbed the rim of a cold barrel right between the eyes of a man who stared up at him from behind the hedge.

Don't make a row! Don't try anything. Just step over, hands up, and do as I tell you."

Silently, the prowler obeyed.

He was a thickset, capable looking character, square-jawed and tough. His eyes never flinched.

Mark dropped the barrel to cover the man's ribs.

"Turn around and walk ahead."

"There's no need for this stuff, Mr. Donovan—"

"Keep going!"

"I am. I know when to take orders. But you're making a mistake—"

"Maybe. In here."

Mark pushed the prisoner into the kitchen, and without removing the gun from his back, bolted the door behind them.

"Straight ahead. Don't make any noise."

His workroom reached, Mark locked the door and, clumsily, went over his captive for arms.

"Under my left arm, Mr. Donovan. There's nothing else."

And, by reason of his unruffled impudence, Mark Donovan became convinced that he had to deal with an agent of Sumuru. He had met others.

He put the man's small automatic down, behind him, and sat on the edge of his desk.

"Turn around now. Let me have a good look at you."

The prisoner obeyed. He was smiling wryly.

"I'm ashamed of myself, Mr. Donovan. But this was a tough assignment. It would have needed one of the old Sioux Indians to shadow that dame in this kind of country!"

When he smiled, the man's grim face lost its roughness. He might have passed for a decent and genial citizen.

"You seem mighty sure of yourself."

"I'm sure of one thing. We're wasting precious time."

Came the sound of a car racing around the drive-way. It pulled up sharply, just outside the study window. Noise of running footsteps followed. Someone was ringing the bell.

Mark glanced from his prisoner to the locked door.

"Go ahead, sir. I won't stir!"

Claudette was coming downstairs.

"Mark! Mark! Someone at the door!"

"Don't go!" he shouted. "Wait for me!"

But he was too late. Claudette had pulled the bolt.

"Stay right where you are. I'm keeping you covered." Mark warned.

He ran to the door, unlocked it and glanced out into the lobby—just as Drake Roscoe stepped in!

IV

"What's all this?" Roscoe snapped, looking from Mark Donovan, raised automatic in hand, to the man he was covering.

"Prisoner, Mr. Roscoe! Just caught him!"

Claudette stifled a cry. Drake Roscoe turned to her, took her arm and drew her forward.

"I'm to blame, Mrs. Donovan, for causing you so much unnecessary anxiety," he assured her. "My excuse—my only excuse—is that I was afraid one of you would give the facts away, unknowingly, to the enemy. Put that gun in your pocket, Donovan!"

"What!"

Mark stared at the face of the man he had captured. The prisoner looked hot and embarrassed.

"This is Kendal Coburn, one of the best agents in the Bureau! He's here on my instructions—has been ever since my first visit!"

"I'm sorry, Mr. Roscoe!" Coburn declared. "That woman spotted me soon after I started. I reported this, you remember? She's as cunning as a weasel. And there's no harder job than tailing in open country."

Claudette reached for Mark's hand, struggling to grasp this totally unexpected new angle.

"Are you talking about—*Anna?*" she asked, her voice hushed.

"I am, ma'am," Coburn acknowledged. "In the beginning, I was covering the little girl. But when, first time, that attractive nurse of yours threw me off the scent, and kept a date with somebody in a Hispano-Suiza—"

"Haven't traced it yet," Roscoe interrupted. "The Duchesse de Severac used a Hispano-Suiza, we have found out, but I suspect it belonged to Miss Finelander. Go ahead, Coburn."

"Yes, please go on!" Claudette whispered.

"Well—I caught up only just in time to see a woman wearing a long, cream-coloured fur coat, talking to your little daughter!"

"Good God!" Mark Donovan grasped his wife's hand tightly.

"Snow mink," Claudette murmured. *"She* always wore mink."

"I watched until this woman stooped and picked the little girl up in her arms. I was all set to run in, when she kissed her and put her back again in her push-car. The Hispano was away before I had a chance to see the plate. There was a second meeting, I believe, but I can't be sure. That foxy Anna of yours doubled on me again. She stuck to a long, straight road and I couldn't find any way to overtake her. When she turned off, I ran to the nearest opening and crossed a field."

He paused, shaking his head.

"Yes, yes, Mr. Coburn?" Claudette prompted.

"I heard a car coming, along the side road. There was a piece of broken wall. I managed to look through. It was the Hispano. I nearly broke cover—for I thought the kid might be in it. Just then, I saw Anna. The baby was with her, laughing and all excited. Unfortunately"—he glanced at Drake Roscoe— "Anna saw *me.*"

"But what happened this evening?" Mark wanted to know.

"I found out, Mr. Donovan, that Anna seemed to get a call—which she took in her own room—every evening after she went off duty."

"I know," Claudette said. "But that was natural enough."

"Quite so, Mrs. Donovan, but I wanted to know more about it. And so, as Mr. Roscoe will tell you, we've been checking all calls in and out of here for some time past. I knew your husband patrolled around sundown, but I thought I could lie behind that hedge and listen to Anna's conversation, as her window was open—"

"What did you hear?"

Claudette's voice was only just audible.

"She was talking to someone she called Caspar. She said she was sure, now, that a police officer or a Federal agent was covering her. And she asked for *instructions*!"

"Go upstairs, *cherie,*" Mark whispered, "and make sure Detty's all right."

Claudette turned and ran out. She was very pale.

"Of course, Roscoe, this call will be traced?" Mark asked.

Drake Roscoe smiled, sourly.

"An earlier one was traced, Donovan. It came from the office of the League of International Fraternity in the Ironstone Building!"

"League of International Fraternity," Mark muttered. "But that's a sort of charity, isn't it?"

"It is. As we're dealing with people who leave few traces, the later calls have been made from Midtown drug-stores! But my time is short. When Mrs. Donovan comes down, ask her to go to Anna's room and invite Anna to take her stockings off! She will know what to look for."

"We have been blind," Mark Donovan groaned. "We had completely dismissed any idea of Sumuru when we came out here. Thought she belonged in Europe. Anna had the highest references—"

"She would have!"

"And Claudette dislikes ugly people about her. So Anna, who is of course a really pretty girl, got the job right away. I must say, she's a model nursemaid. Patient, intelligent, and highly cultured." He clenched his fists. "Good God! *how* blind we've been!"

"You realize," Roscoe said, "that it will be impossible to arrest this girl? We have nothing on her whatever! But she must leave at once, and I'll see that she's covered to wherever she goes. Now that you know one another, I should be glad if you could find a shakedown for Coburn. I want him to stay in the house until I return."

"Shall you be gone long?" Donovan asked anxiously.

"Probably not. I'm flying to Miami by special plane tonight. Ah! here's your wife."

Claudette came in, a bewildered expression on her beautiful face.

"Is Detty all right?" Mark asked.

"Yes, dear. I found her dozing off quite peacefully. When I kissed her, she whispered 'booful lady' and went sound asleep. But—"

"We want you," Mark spoke urgently, "to go along to Anna's room—"

"I have been!"

"What's that?" Drake Roscoe rapped out the words.

"It's what I came to tell you—Anna has gone!"

"Gone?"

"The drawers are all turned out, but she can't have taken half her things. And the kitchen door is wide open."

Drake Roscoe and Coburn exchanged glances.

"Too late!" Roscoe said. "A thousand to a peanut she received her 'instructions' right after Mr. Donovan interrupted you. They knew she was spotted before she reported it. A car will be standing by to get her away." He glanced at his watch. "I must be off. Keep a sharp lookout, Coburn."

CHAPTER ELEVEN

I

And down in Florida, at a late hour that night, Tony McKeigh opened his eyes and stared across a small room at a man who sat facing him.

This room puzzled him at first. It was low-roofed, rectangular and panelled in light wood. There were two shuttered windows. An upholstered sofa ran right along one side under the windows, and there were two deep, comfortable armchairs, in one of which he was seated. A shaded wall-lamp gave the only illumination. The floor was thickly carpeted.

In the other armchair a man sat watching him.

A movement which he had thought to be imaginary, and associated with a vague nausea, he suddenly recognized to be real.

He was in the cabin of some small vessel.

But even these simple details came to him vaguely. He was held by the fixed regard of the man who sat there watching him.

This man, who wore a perfectly cut white linen suit, had a profusion of dark hair, greying slightly at the temples. His features were good, but Tony felt that he would like to see more clearly the eyes behind tinted glasses.

They appeared to be focused intently upon him, but as he revived, the disconcerting focus was altered. The man spoke.

"I fear you have had an alarming experience, Mr. McKeigh."

It was a cultured voice, softly modulated.

McKeigh swallowed, experimentally, and replied, "Yes. The facts are not clear to me yet."

"Footpads are a novelty in Fort Lauderdale—if a commonplace in London. I acted only just in time. I ventured to apply a simple restorative. Perhaps you would check your property and see if anything is missing."

Automatically, McKeigh obeyed. Two things were missing: his notebook, with notes in code, and his wallet.

"Your wallet I have here, if that is what you are looking for. I took the liberty of searching for a card in order to learn your identity."

The wallet was extended to him. Tony McKeigh stood up and took it. A glance inside convinced him that its contents were intact.

"Thanks. Nothing missing but my notebook—although I'd rather they'd taken everything else and left me my notes."

"Indeed. Your notes concerning the private life of Steve Mason, no doubt?"

And at that, a sudden suspicion took hold of Tony McKeigh, and for the second time on that eventful night, his spine tingled coldly.

His earlier theory, that he had been spotted by agents of Steve Mason, must have been correct. Mason meant to keep his hiding-place a secret. And Sumuru? He was certain it was to Sumuru he had been talking. Where did *she* fit in? Had she led him into the trap? For beyond any shadow of doubt, he had walked right into one.

He must play safe until the facts of his situation became clearer, and until he had overcome this unpleasant swimmy sensation. Also, he must conquer an uncanny obsession—an idea that there was someone else in the cabin—that he was not *alone* with this man.

"Just so," he said casually. "You seem to be well informed."

"It is my business to be well informed. My name is Vanderson—Carl Vanderson. I represent the Ned W. Regan Detective Bureau."

"Oh, really!" Tony McKeigh was honestly surprised. "You are acting for Mason, I suppose?"

He was conscious of a certain sense of relief. But he decided that he could never like Mr. Carl Vanderson.

"You are assuming, I suppose, that Mason's thugs nobbled you—is that good colloquial English? Well, such things do occur. But you are also assuming that they did so with my knowledge. You are wrong. I heard the sound of the fracas and came to your assistance. You are on board Mr. Charles Madderley's motor cruiser."

The man's voice was without emotion; almost without humanity. And it had an authoritative tone which McKeigh found hard to put up with.

"I am greatly obliged to you, Mr. Vanderson. My sincere thanks."

Mr. Vanderson was watching him again. And again Tony was touched by that ghostly obsession of another listener.

"The catastrophe called Steve Mason may be likened to a plague of locusts, or to an epidemic. Mason is not the first petty dictator to attempt to blackmail a whole country into submitting to his will. (You may recall the name of Huey Long?) He will not be the last. He imposed, temporarily, conditions upon the United States which wise Americans will never forget. No section of the community stands to lose more if Steve Masons are permitted to exist, than labour, of which he poses as a champion."

"H'm," McKeigh murmured, "I see you're no lover of Steve's."

"I am not—although he retained our services recently. But I am interested to learn that his activities seem of sufficient importance to a London newspaper to justify a visit to Florida."

"They do!" Tony saw that he had to regularize his appearance in Lauderdale. "We have Steve Masons and similar squirps in high places in Britain, and we haven't found out yet how to deal with them!"

"Indeed? Yet such men have their uses—under proper direction. The man Mason has a bull-like force which we, for instance, could employ to good purpose. Therefore, I do not desire his death."

The unemotional tones never varied. The speaker used perfect, or rather, exact English; yet McKeigh could tell that he was not an Englishman.

"Is there any likelihood of his death?" he asked.

"I doubt if even I can save him."

There was godlike assumption in that statement, a clear implication that the speaker (or the Ned W. Regan Bureau) was the last court of appeal.

"Do you mean that he suffers from some incurable disease?"

"Undoubtedly. Vanity."

McKeigh was becoming his own man again. He remained bewildered, but no longer afraid. Why should this unusual specimen of a private eye confide these singular facts to a stranger?

"Does vanity kill?"

"Yes; it blinds its victim to danger."

"You mean that someone plans to murder Mason?"

"I mean just that."

Like an echo, so strangely true it was, Tony McKeigh seemed to hear a voice which sometimes touched the notes of a silver bell:

"I should propose to remove the leprous source of such haemorrhages ..."

His brain grew vitally alert. What was afoot? To which party did this man, Vanderson, really belong? Was he here to protect Steve Mason? And did he know that he was opposed to the secret power of Sumuru? Above all—where *was* Mason?

A mental image of the brawny agitator arose before him. He saw that figure, familiarized by press photographers, self-confident, loud-spoken, surrounded by a bodyguard of trained thugs; a vulgar Alexander with a new world to conquer. And so, when he answered, he spoke guardedly.

"Not so easy, I should say. Four of his crew resigned without notice recently, it's true; but he has Federal protection, and also, he has retained your services."

"My dear Mr. McKeigh! He has been marked down by the second of the two first-class brains in the world to-day. The official police of this entire country, supported by all the private agencies, could not save him!"

"This is hard to believe."

"You find it so? Yet all our resources—and they are considerable—have not enabled us to establish contact with Mason. But the presence of a certain person at the Madderley home, her method of leaving, and your own recent experience, point to the fact that Mason is there. He is Jane Madderley's lover. He has grasped the reality of his danger. He has fled from it. But a first-class brain has almost magical powers."

"Who owns this phenomenal 'grey'?"

"A woman."

"What?"

McKeigh had almost decided that Mr. Carl Vanderson was an unusual type of lunatic, but now he found himself interested, curious, wildly stimulated. Beyond doubt, he knew that woman!

"A woman of quite uncommon beauty, and that most dangerous of all creatures, a fanatic of genius. And now, Mr. McKeigh, as you seem quite restored, I will see you ashore."

II

Steve Mason, his heavy-jowled, beetle-browed face (a face to have made any sculptor cast aside mallet and chisel) set in deep lines of despair, paced up and down a shuttered and draped bedroom. His massive frame seemed to have shrunk. His great shoulders were stooped. The wildness of his eyes touched the point of ferocity. He resembled a bear newly captured.

And, standing watching him, in that gaily furnished room, her hands clasped convulsively over her breast, was a woman, dark-eyed, handsome, and shapely to excess; normally vivacious, but now on the verge of hysteria.

"Where else should I come, Jane?" he growled. "If I'm not safe with you, where am I safe?"

She made no reply, only continued to watch him with those haunted dark eyes. He pulled up in front of her, snatched her clasped hands apart and held her helpless in his grip.

"You don't love me any more! That's it! What's the bastard's name?"

"Steve! Steve!"

"Never mind 'Steve, Steve!' Who is it?"

"Steve! Someone will hear you—"

The flame of anger, desire, jealousy, whatever it was, flickered out of him. He relaxed his grasp and resumed that pacing up and down. The woman shrank nearer to the door. Mason began to talk at random. He always talked at random, trusting to the torrent of words to carry him along until he hit something. Political reputations are often made like that.

"All my life—all my life—I give to the cause of labour. Every day of it since I can think. Every hour that I'm not asleep. It's a holy thing, it's a sacred thing—the toil of men's hands..."

He was just turning the engines over, and after a lot of churning:

"When I get a tight hold, when I show 'em that what I ask for I can take just as easy if they say no—what happens?" he demanded.

"It happened before that, Steve," the woman whispered. "I warned you it would happen—"

Steve Mason checked his bear patrol. He kicked away a litter of newspapers which lay at his feet. They carried front page headlines with the query: "Where is Steve Mason?" or variations on

109

the same theme. He turned savage eyes in Jane Madderley's direction.

"*You* warned me?" He moved towards her. "*You* warned me! What in hell did *you* know about it?"

"I knew"—she faced up to him— "that you shouldn't have called the strike. That racket had been tried before, and failed. Then I knew your only chance would be to call it off."

He was standing right in front of her, his great jaw protruded so that it nearly touched her rounded chin.

"*You* knew!" he rumbled. "*You* did! How did you know? Who was putting you wise? If I thought—" He clenched his powerful fists, but Jane never flinched. "Was it Charlie?"

"I knew just by instinct."

"Instinct, eh? Perhaps you know by instinct who sends me messages telling me where and how soon I get off—"

"All public men get those messages."

"Do they? Do they get some damn' voice calling 'em up middle of the night and counting out the hours they got left to live? Do they find gold-lettered cards laying on the breakfast table with the same thing in print, and nobody put 'em there?"

He paused to recover breath to go on again. He began to kick the newspapers, individually and severally, into remote corners of the room.

"I figure I'm marked down. Don't know who by. So I get protection. Four of the guys I employ just disappear one night. It gets me cold—and I'm not pretending it doesn't. And when I sneak down here to Florida like a bum on the run, what do I find? A bloody great party! The house full of cissies!"

"How was I to know you were coming, Steve?

But he ignored her.

"Sneaked in like something contagious and hid in your goddam bedroom. What's going on? And where's Charlie?"

"He's in New York—thank heaven!"

"Let him stop there. But I can't stay here—living like a bloody canary!"

"You shouldn't have come! Oh, my God, you shouldn't have come!"

He turned on her in swift fury.

"Now I have it straight! Now it's plain! Now I know where I get off! I'm an intruder. Charlie's a prominent citizen of this dump. It was good fun to have Steve Mason tailing after you like a French poodle while he held the United States in his two fists. But now he's been punished badly and counted out, he's not so hot, eh? Fine!"

He kicked an unoffending newspaper supplement from side to side of the room—and a square card with gold lettering fell out.

When he turned his eyes in Jane's direction again, they were suffused, red. And all the stiffening had gone out of Steve Mason. He was limp.

"Get me my reading-glasses," he directed hoarsely. "In the suit-case."

Jane Madderley moved in obedience.

There was something in his criticism, but not everything. A woman of dominant personality, who ruled Charles Madderley, her husband, with a threat disguised as a smile, the celebrated labour boss, Steve Mason, had begun by offending her. Later, it had been amusing to tame this savage beast.

Then had come orders to cage him.

They were orders she dared not dream of disobeying, but orders which terrified her. She had tried to delude herself with the hope that Our Lady had forgiven and forgotten her. Now, out of a clear sky, came evidence to prove that she had not. To the end of her days she would belong to the Order, be one of "The Women"... and she knew that the death of Celie Artz (whom she had once known as Sister Celeste) was no "love tragedy" as reported in the newspapers.

It was an agonizing situation; for, at last, Jane Madderley knew she had met her master in Steve Mason. She had surrendered, unconditionally. Lately, she had begun to resent his coarse acceptance of a broken pride, but—

"They are not here."

Her voice had sunk to a whisper. She was trembling.

"Let me look. What's bitten you? Scared?"

Savagely, Mason turned out the contents of the case. If as he did so, he could have seen Jane's face, he might have learned something; for it was the face of a woman suffering the pangs of damnation. The moment had come. She had her orders—but she distrusted their purpose. It seemed harmless enough, yet...

"Hell! I had 'em with me!"

"Don't shout, Steve. Try to be calm. They're just mislaid—maybe in the car. You left a spare pair here, last time you flew down. I'll get them."

"Did I? Wait a minute. Read this thing out to me." The hairy hand clutching the card was shaking. "I don't give a damn—but read me what it says. How it got here, *you* have to find out. Read it."

And in a voice which she forced to a steady monotone, Jane Madderley read:

"Your resignation as president of the union has not been announced. Make your peace with God—if you believe in a hereafter. La Femme."

"Get my glasses," Mason whispered. "Let *me* read it—"

III

When Tony McKeigh stepped ashore, accompanied by the suave but supercilious Mr. Vanderson, he found himself close to the spot where he had been so mysteriously attacked. He turned to Vanderson.

"Why is the Madderley cruiser tied up so far from home?" he asked, looking back at the handsome craft he had just left.

"Their own dock is under repair, I believe. But you haven't far to go, if you intend to visit Mrs. Madderley. Keep straight on and then take the last turning but one. Or perhaps, after your unpleasant experience, you prefer to get back to your hotel?"

"Thanks," Tony answered dryly. "I'll think about it. Going my way?"

"I have to return on board. I'm waiting for a vital report from my assistant, who is covering the house. Good night, Mr. McKeigh. So sorry about your notes."

Tony watched the tall, athletic figure step lithely back on to the craft and disappear into the darkened cabin.

He looked up at the moon, a silver mirror in a velvet sky. The breeze had dropped. Palm fronds might have been carved out of ebony, so starkly they showed against the blue. How long had elapsed since that conversation with the woman whose voice was seductive music?

Not a moving figure showed in sight. Except for faint whispering of tidal water, the night seemed uncannily still.

He started to walk rapidly towards the Madderley home. He began to regret that he wasn't armed. Carl Vanderson was not a person to inspire confidence, although the famous detective agency to which he belonged enjoyed the highest reputation.

His behaviour wasn't consistent. Why should he put a man ashore, a man who had suffered a murderous attack, and leave him alone to face a possible second assault? This, particularly, didn't make sense in the case of a representative of the Ned W. Regan Bureau.

A car was heading his way—a car that carried a searchlight.

There was no cover. If this meant Sumuru, he had walked right into her hands!

The speeding automobile pulled up, with a screeching of brakes. Tony McKeigh saw the word "Police".

And Drake Roscoe jumped out and ran to him!

IV

Our Lady lolled on the cushioned settee of the cabin cruiser from which Tony McKeigh had so recently gone ashore. Her snow mink stole had dropped from her shoulders. She was smoking a cigarette in a black onyx holder. Ariost stood before her, his hands clenched.

"I must repeat, Madonna, it is madness! Apart from the fact that police may board us at any moment, what do we know of Roscoe's information? He may be acquainted with all Regan's operatives. They work close to the F.B.I. if jealously. The danger is too great. It is tempting fate."

Sumuru smiled, extended a perfect arm and touched Ariosto's hand with caressing fingers.

"You speak of fate—Kismet, the Arabs call it. Kismet rules *us,* my friend. We do not rule Kismet. You speak of danger. What fire is there in life without danger? I have exposed myself to that delightful fire to-night. At this moment, the London journalist will know that he has met the woman they call Sumuru—which reminds me of something. What do you think of this Tony McKeigh?"

"Physically, he is a good specimen. His brain is sound, but his mind is frivolous."

"You mean he is young? No matter. We digress. Excuse a woman's whim. As you, alone, are responsible for the project which brings us to Florida to-night, it rests with you to ensure its success. We must leave no evidence. You have the duplicate. Therefore, you must go—"

"Madonna!" It was almost a groan.

113

"Must I say it is an order, Ariosto? Or do you go to please me?"

Ariosto stooped, raised Sumuru's hand to his lips, then turned and went out.

V

The Madderley cocktail party had broken up earlier than usual; for frequent absences of the vivacious hostess, and her pre-occupation whenever she joined her guests, had cast a wet blanket over nearly everybody.

It was common ground amongst the scandalmongers (and those who frequent cocktail parties generally prefer scandal to Manhattans) that Jane was worried about Steve Mason. Nobody even suggested that she might be worried about her husband. But at one-forty-five, Jane being missing, there are a few serious drinkers (of the sturdy type which ignores outside interference) still hard at work.

They had a shock coming.

At approximately one-fifty, Drake Roscoe, Tony McKeigh, and a party of armed police walked into the big lounge-hall. Roscoe, his brown face set grimly, looked around.

"Don't be alarmed. Just stay right where you are. Where is Mrs. Madderley?"

He was told, upstairs.

He turned to the police lieutenant who had accompanied him. "Stand by, here. Come on, Mac."

And he went racing up the wide stairway.

The first door which Drake Roscoe threw open without ceremony was that of Jane Madderley's bedroom—and there they came face to face with Steve Mason!

His high colour had gone, giving place to a leaden pallor. His lips moved, but no words came. He raised both hands automatically, at sight of the intruders—then jabbed a quivering finger in the direction of an inner door. There was slight froth on his lips.

Drake Roscoe merely nodded and, ignoring Mason, pushed open the door indicated. McKeigh entered behind him.

"Good God!" he exclaimed.

This was an ornate boudoir, lighted only by a violet-shaded lamp beside a lacquer writing cabinet. And seated there, facing them as they entered, he saw Jane Madderley. She wore a pair of

114

thick-rimmed spectacles, and her dark eyes stared straight before her sightlessly.

She was quite motionless, quite expressionless—and quite dead.

Both Roscoe and McKeigh were so stunned by the discovery that they failed to hear a third man enter almost at their heels—until he spoke.

"Ah! I'm too late! You will have noted, Mr. McKeigh, and I trust you will faithfully report, the amazing resources of a first-class brain."

Drake Roscoe twisted around in a flash. He stood staring.

"This is Carl Vanderson," Tony McKeigh spoke automatically. "Of the Ned Regan Bureau."

Vanderson bowed coldly. He still wore the tinted glasses and the white suit, to which, Tony McKeigh noted, he had added a pair of immaculate white gloves.

"At your service. Mr. Drake Roscoe, I believe—acting under direct instructions from Washington? Mr. McKeigh I have already had the privilege of meeting. I may explain that Mr. Mason is a client of our bureau. I fear that my confrere has ruined our reputation."

He crossed, calmly, stooped over the dead woman, and removed the spectacles she was wearing! For when he turned to Drake Roscoe, he held them in his gloved hand.

"I am going to leave this evidence with you, Mr. Roscoe." He passed the glasses to Drake Roscoe. "You are the proper person to hold it. You know, as we know, with whom we are dealing. You call the head of the organization Sumuru—the name by which she is known to London's Scotland Yard. So do we, for we know no other."

"We know several others!" Drake Roscoe growled. "This case is no advertisement for the Regan Bureau!"

"I admit it. But you, also, came too late? Your deductions will be the same as mine. Jane Madderley, I assume, was one of the many slaves of this amazing woman. You agree with me? In some way—perhaps as others have done—she failed to carry out her orders—"

Tony McKeigh was thinking hard, but he said nothing yet.

"Or she bungled them. Jane Madderley illustrates the weakness of any feminine campaign. She loved Steve Mason."

"Maybe," Tony McKeigh broke in. "But what, according to your deductions, were the orders she bungled?"

"To substitute other reading-glasses for his own. We shall find the pair he wore, habitually, hidden somewhere in these apartments."

"What was the object?" Roscoe demanded harshly, looking down at the glasses he held.

"His death! Sumuru has failed. The Bureau has met with this method before. You see, we keep abreast of scientific developments! Those lenses (you have nothing to fear from them now) were radio-active! The process is a secret. Its full properties have yet to be learned, and the name of its inventor. All we know—there have been two former cases—is that it has power to destroy life, leaving no trace. In darkness it is harmless. For a period of a few minutes, only, it becomes, on exposure to light—deadly."

"And what do you deduce from the fact that Mrs. Madderley and not Steve Mason, was wearing these glasses?"

"That she doubted the real object of her orders, and tried them on, herself." Drake Roscoe laid the glasses on a table. He faced Carl Vanderson.

"Mr. Vanderson," he said, "you are a damnably clever fellow!"

Carl Vanderson smiled. It was an oddly nervous smile for so self-assured a character.

"But the Bureau has given me a damnably dumb assistant!" he assured Roscoe. "The fool is downstairs. I will bring him up to meet you. Quick analysis of those lenses may yield some result— but I doubt it. Excuse me for a moment."

Carl Vanderson went out, a handsome figure in his well-cut suit. He had passed the doorway, passed Steve Mason slumped in an armchair, gone down the stairs, when Tony McKeigh spoke.

"Roscoe! Roscoe! There's something wrong here! That man claims to have rescued me, but—"

Drake Roscoe frowned, ran to the door.

"Lieutenant Olsen!"

"Sir!"

"Ask Mr. Vanderson to step upstairs again."

There was a pause, and then came:

"The man from Regan's?"

"Yes."

"He left—just this minute!"

CHAPTER TWELVE
I

"My compliments, Ariosto, upon your sleight-of-hand. You were always expert. Your recovery of the radioactive glasses and substitution of others was admirable."

"Thanks to insulated gloves, Madonna."

"Naturally. And you escaped out of the lion's den. I must really congratulate you."

Sumuru lay back in her seat, watching him under lowered lashes. Her mink stole had fallen from her shoulders. Light from a lamp beside her enhanced the satin of bare shoulders. She was smoking. The plane flew at a high altitude, and Miami already was far behind.

Ariosto, seated facing her, glanced at the shadowed eyes, and then glanced away again.

"We nearly made a fatal mistake, Madonna."

"*Nearly,* did I understand you to say, my friend?"

"The police will have boarded the *Laguna,* and have found out to whom the boat belongs," Ariosto went on doggedly. "This can only lead to dangerous inquiries. Not only the man McKeigh, but now, also, Drake Roscoe could identify me at any time."

Sumuru knocked ash from the tip of her cigarette.

"Equally, both could identify *me* at any time," she murmured musically.

"You are not one woman, but many women. You have an alibi to disprove any charge that can be laid against you. Our Lady is infallible."

"It pleases you to be ironical, Ariosto. Your distaste for danger seems to stimulate a spurious insolence. You dare to tell me to my face that I am infallible when I have just failed to carry out a plan matured over months of study. I now tell you, Ariosto, that you are a pitiful bungler!" In anger, her tones didn't rise, they fell to an icy whisper. "Always, I distrusted this new device of yours. It leaves too much to chance.

Ariosto clenched his fists. His dark eyes were burning with repressed passion.

"The chance was one about which I warned you. Success or failure lay in the hands of Sister Juno—in the hands of a woman in love!"

"In which event, she deserved to die.... That one of *my* women should give her heart to Steve Mason! Here, indeed, is black failure! Celeste dealt a dreadful blow to my pride, and now—another. Is my dream of elevating woman to the place in society which belongs to her, to end in smoke? Am I the only woman of them all who can keep lovers in their place? What is this madness—shared, Ariosto, by few men—which urges some women to sacrifice everything for the myth they call 'love'?"

"Always, Madonna, always I distrusted her."

Sumuru shrugged, indolently.

"So you have mentioned before. But why change the subject? She has failed me—but paid the price. As a physician, what is your opinion of the man, Steve Mason?"

Ariosto stifled his anger to consider the question.

"His nerve already was broken. The death of Mrs. Madderley—Sister Juno—has led to a mental collapse. He will probably survive it. But we have nothing to fear from him for a long time."

Sumuru's eyes closed entirely.

"Arrange a consultation, my friend. Your standing in New York is high. I have looked to this. He will almost certainly accept an offer from the Finelander Foundation Sanitarium to rest there under expert supervision. See that he rests... for good."

Ariosto's fine forehead glistened in the subdued light, as if suddenly damp.

"I shall do my best to carry out Madonna's wishes."

"To me, the best means fulfilment."

"Your wishes shall be fulfilled, Madonna."

"It is so simple," she murmured softly. "When we penetrate the Iron Curtain—you will have more difficult problems. The man Mason is a mere exercise."

There followed some moments of tense silence, and then—

"Drake Roscoe is unpleasantly well informed," Ariosto said. "I had not expected to meet him to-night. I thought I had to deal only with his assistant, who is a mere amateur."

Sumuru's eyes remained closed. She made no reply for a long time.

"Drake Roscoe," came, at last, and there was music in the way she spoke the name, "begins to interest me..."

II

"No, Mr. McKeigh, we have no Carl Vanderson on our pay-roll. I may add, that Mr. Steve Mason has never briefed us. Your description of the impostor doesn't help much. There are thousands of men who look something like that walking around Manhattan."

This was the information with which Tony McKeigh came away from the offices of the Ned W. Regan Detective Bureau. It had been anticipated. His visit was a mere routine check-up.

The motor-cruiser *Laguna* had turned out to belong to a Mrs. Franklyn Delabole, resident during the winter months in Palm Beach. She, and her cousin, Willis Delabole, (who looked after the *Laguna)* had run down to dine with friends in Fort Lauderdale on the night of Mrs. Madderley's tragic death.

Mrs. Delabole declared that she had no idea of the identity of the man who claimed to have rescued Tony, and that certainly he had had no authority to be on board. She didn't know the Madderleys.

("But I'd bet," had been Roscoe's grim comment, "she knows Sumuru!")

Every immediate source of inquiry seemed to be sealed up. Miss Rhoda Finelander and her secretary were visiting in Virginia. Drake Roscoe had wasted valuable hours driving out to Connecticut to interview the lady. A perfect old English butler had shown him every courtesy, suggested sherry and biscuits, and assured him that he knew nothing of the history of the hulk, *John P. Faraway,* except that Miss Finelander had, at one time, the idea of converting the craft to the purposes of a sea-going yacht.

"Her failing health, sir," he had pointed out, sadly, "may have led to a change of plan."

Wheels within wheels. People of high social status apparently tied up with this Order, which seemed to include every grade of humanity.

Tony McKeigh was considering these things and regarding the prospects of success for Drake Roscoe in a more and more dim light as he walked along.

Sumuru's resources were truly formidable. Either she was the Duchesse de Severac or the Duchesse was her stout supporter. The wealth of the Finelanders apparently backed her American enterprises. And it was reasonable to assume that she had similarly important friends all over the world.

Roscoe was so fully convinced that Sumuru meant to get possession of the Donovans' child that he had induced the anxious parents to take a European vacation and had pulled official wires to fix them, at short notice, in the *Queen Elizabeth,* leaving in two days.

Sumuru had the power to change the course of human lives...

Tony McKeigh's route led him past the Grand Central entrance, but he remained too deep in thought to be interested in arriving travellers until a porter opened the door of a Cadillac and a girl got out who wore a mink coat. She wore no hat, so that even from behind he couldn't mistake the gleam of that wavy hair.

It was Viola Stayton!

At the very moment that the porter took out a light suitcase and put the case down beside her, Tony grasped Viola's arm. His heart was galloping, but he kept his voice steady.

"Don't try any drama, Viola. Just pretend you expected me."

Viola turned in a flash. Her glance avoided him, and he saw her grow pale.

"What are you going to do?" she whispered.

"Pick up your suitcase, tell your chauffeur to push off, and pack you into a taxi!"

"But—it's impossible—"

The chauffeur sat regarding him without interest, and didn't seem inclined to interfere. Tony congratulated himself on a natural performance, but wondered at the same time where he had seen the chauffeur before. The porter had moved off to attend to another customer.

"It doesn't have to be, Viola. If you won't come quietly, as the London constables say, I'm going to take your advice. Remember?"

"No."

"I'm going to start calling for a policeman—and this time I shall mean it!"

Viola's expression, he found impossible to define. Already he was puzzling over the future, trying to imagine how he could save her, from Sumuru, from herself if necessary, and from justice.

She flashed him one swift, ambiguous glance, and then dropped her lashes.

"There's nothing I can say."

Tony nodded. "Dismiss your driver," he told her tersely.

Viola turned to the dark-faced chauffeur.

"You needn't wait, Sanchez. Mr. McKeigh will look after me." As the man, his features immobile as those of a mask, touched his cap and drove off: "Don't bother about the number," she added to Tony. "The Cadillac doesn't belong to Our Lady."

"As far as I can make out," he answered drily, "Our Lady seems to get along very nicely without having to buy anything for herself!" He opened the door of a taxi which he had signalled. "Jump in."

Putting the suitcase on the floor, he got in beside Viola.

"Where are you taking me?"

"Savoy Babylon," he called to the driver.

Then he drew a deep breath, lay back, and looked at his prisoner. She was certainly well worth the trouble. In fact, he found her so lovely that she made his head swim. He didn't quite know how to open a conversation. He took out his cigarette case.

"Won't you smoke, Viola?"

She shook her head. And the way light danced on her hair made him long to bury his face in its rippling waves, as once—it seemed an age ago—he had done. He lighted one for himself.

"This tobacco isn't doped, you know," he informed her, lightly.

Still she didn't look at him, but:

"Why do you say that?" she asked.

"You should know! You kindly added something to my pipe tobacco the last time I met you! I'm sure it was the tobacco, because we have worked out you couldn't have handled my glass."

Viola was silent for a long time.

"Don't you remember anything after that?" she inquired at last.

"No!" Tony lied. "Nothing that I believe really happened."

"But what do you remember, whether it really happened or not?"

Tony McKeigh's arm stole round behind her shoulders.

"I thought I was floating away up in space and looking down at my dead body. There was a woman beside me, down there, but it wasn't you."

"Who was it?" Viola asked quickly.

Tony checked himself just in time. There was grim evidence to show that those who knew too much about Sumuru didn't live long. His fingers were caressing the soft fur.

"A stranger. When I really woke up, there was no one there at all." He tightened his clasp slightly. "This is a beautiful coat you're wearing, Viola."

Viola laughed, quite unmirthfully.

"We all receive one, on being accepted."

"Really? I shall probably find myself in trouble if I stop to inspect the ankles of every woman wearing mink I happen to come across!"

Viola persistently stared out of the off-side window, as if fascinated by the spectacle of Park Avenue on a sunny morning.

"Why should you inspect their ankles?"

He was holding her tightly now. All Sumuru's women have a faint mark on one ankle—a sort of tattooed slave bangle. It means that they belong, for all their lives, to 'Our Lady,' doesn't it?"

He felt her shudder. They may not think of it as a slave bangle. They may be proud of it." She lifted her coat and raised one slim ankle gracefully. "Please inspect *me*. Because you might as well know."

Tony McKeigh inspected, with intense but restrained interest. Under a spider-web stocking he could just detect the faint outline of a snake holding its tail in its mouth. As the raised foot was lowered:

"You have adorably pretty legs," he murmured.

He saw Viola flush as she averted her face again.

"And I suppose I must consider myself under arrest?"

"That's up to Roscoe, darling. And I *do* remember something else—whether it really happened or not ..."

III

"It chances," Drake Roscoe said thoughtfully, "that two rooms and bath, adjoining, which complete this suite, the rest of which I use, became vacant to-day." He stared hard at Viola. "You will occupy those quarters until further notice. Any comment?"

She shook her head, glanced at Tony McKeigh.

"I could clap you straight in jail," Roscoe added. "We have quite enough evidence. Your acrobatic antics in this very room—to which McKeigh, here, can bear witness—alone would justify it. But I hope, to bring you to your senses. This woman Sumuru, whom you call 'Our Lady', is a big-time gangster. Sooner or later, we'll have her in Sing Sing. Think it over. But take my advice. Get out while the going's good."

He took up the phone.

Viola had undergone an examination lasting nearly an hour. I Drake Roscoe had never failed in reasonable courtesy to the prisoner, except for one outburst when he had exclaimed, "The hell with this business! I'm not a blasted district attorney!" But he had seen the wisdom of keeping Viola incommunicado, and the possible use to be made of Tony McKeigh in this situation.

She had given the name and address of her father without hesitation: Colonel Gerald Stayton, of Old Hall, Warwickshire, England. She said she was the youngest of three sisters and that her life in America gave her father no cause for anxiety. Her duties allowed her to correspond with him regularly.

On the subject of these duties she remained silent. She declined to state her place of residence in Manhattan. She said she had never heard the name Sumuru. She admitted that she belonged to the Order of Our Lady, but declared that it was a league dedicated to the betterment of mankind.

What was the real identity of "Our Lady," she was asked.

Viola replied that neither she nor any other member knew.

A buzz at the door announced a visitor. Tony McKeigh admitted a capable-looking young woman, fresh coloured and smartly dressed. Drake Roscoe crossed to meet her.

"This lady"—he indicated Viola— "will be your responsibility, Miss Rorke. She will occupy Apartment 365—next to mine. Her baggage—one suitcase—is there in the lobby. So please take care of her." He glanced at Viola. "I shall be seeing you later, Miss Stayton."

When the two had gone out:

"Who's Miss Rorke?" Tony McKeigh inquired.

"A woman detective from Headquarters. She's cultured and competent—but as hard-boiled as they come if there's any trouble."

He began to pace up and down, restlessly.

Tony McKeigh remained torn between rapture and self-contempt. He was lost, irrevocably lost, and he knew it. Merely to be near Viola meant the wildest happiness; her touch thrilled every nerve in his body. Those old romances in which men bartered their lives, their souls, for the love of an adored but unworthy woman he had rejected as absurd. He still thought them absurd—which was why he despised himself.

He suppressed a sigh.

"What are your plans, Roscoe? You're not built for beating-up unwilling witnesses. D'you think there's any way to make her talk?"

Roscoe shot a steely glance in Tony's direction.

"Not for *me* to make her talk, short of racks and thumb-screws. But she may talk *to you!*"

Tony McKeigh felt a flush creeping over his face.

"That puts me in a very delicate spot."

"A spot of your own making. I didn't ask you to fall in love with her. For that matter, I didn't ask you to bring her *here.*"

"I thought that was my plain duty. What should I have done—let her go?"

Drake Roscoe pulled up short.

"No. Come to think of it, I don't see what else you could have done. But, all the same, I have an unpleasant feeling that we've made a wrong move. Dealing with this woman Sumuru, seems to develop an extra sense."

"An extra sense is needed! I'm not likely to forget strolling along with her ladyship in Fort Lauderdale until we reached the spot where I suppose she had planned to throw me in."

"I have a different theory, Mac. You were never intended to be drowned—-only to be kept out of the way until the plot to liqui-date Steve Mason had been completed. We know, now, that the man calling himself Vanderson was one of Sumuru's people. They all share a common attribute—brazen audacity."

Tony McKeigh recalled Viola's overtaking him on the street, to give him the wallet; her climb down into Drake Roscoe's apartment; her visit to himself—and what she had come for. He felt suddenly sick at heart.

Viola was part of an organization whose ideology treated murder lightly. And she had him hopelessly bewitched.

"Whatever your personal feelings may be," Drake Roscoe went on, "and whatever the outcome, you must do your damnedest to get certain facts out of this girl. She's well educated and well born. Youth is often blind to truth. Think of her as a victim, and do all that's possible. The stakes are too high to let sentiment standing in your way."

Tony cleared his throat, nervously.

"Shouldn't we check on inhabitants of apartment above?" he asked, some of his usual jaunty manner fighting through. "Thinking of the acrobatic feats you mentioned."

"Detective-Officer Rorke has orders to screw the windows down, and whenever she goes out to lock the door. I haven't forgotten that 'Our Lady' has a long arm."

IV

Our Lady was stretched on the mink-covered divan in a relaxed and graceful attitude. She wore her favourite indoor dress on this occasion of pale violet, so that the curves of her pliant body gleamed through the gossamer as if through the mist of an Eastern sunset. The silver mosque lamps were lighted and the air was heavy with perfume of mimosa. That tent-like room, the woman on the divan and no sound but the plashing of water in the pond, suggested the pavilion of a sultan's favourite.

Caspar, his face a smiling ivory mask, stood there, head bowed. But his lowered glance secretly traced each line of Sumuru's perfect shape; and Caspar, alone, knew what Caspar was thinking.

"Sanchez followed them to the Savoy Babylon, My Lady—"

"I know all this. Why weary me with repetitions?"

Caspar bowed even more deeply.

"The apartment so long occupied, as My Lady directed—"

"Was vacated this morning. How tedious you are to-day, Caspar. Do you imagine I am so indolent that I wait for *you* to give me these summaries of reports?" She leaned on one elbow, looking up. "Or do you waste my time so that you can feast your old eyes on my beauty?"

"My Lady is angry."

"If this boyish curiosity, sometimes recurring in second childhood, is not sufficiently satisfied, perhaps you would care to attend me in the bath to-night? I could dismiss Bella and you might hold my robe while I swim." She lay back again, and smiled. "But I am slandering you. I had forgotten that you came to me from Mohammed al-Akra. Your duties, I recall, included assessing the value of slaves to be offered for sale, at Mecca and elsewhere. Tell me, Caspar, do you think I should command a good price?"

127

"My Lady jests! There is no man in the East to-day whose entire treasury could meet such a price."

For that compliment, I forgive you. But only because it is true. You have been with me longer than any of them, Caspar Have you sometimes asked yourself why I never change? Have you asked yourself if I might be the Wandering Jewess?"

Caspar's hands closed, convulsively.

"No, for you are not a Jewess, Madonna."

"But I *wander*! You have wandered with me—on—and on—and on."

She laughed, that bubbling, joyous laughter like the muted song of a skylark. Taking up the ostrich fan which lay beside her, she brushed Caspar's lowered eyes with the white plume.

He met her glance, for a moment only.

"You have known me long enough to know when I am teasing you, Caspar. One thing, only, I wait to learn, my friend: Does Sister Viola occupy the apartment next to Drake Roscoe?"

"She does, My Lady."

"Good. And now, Caspar, some fruit, wheat cakes, and a flask of the Cyprian wine—although I fear my poor wine has suffered in transit to this barbarous country. Hurry, Caspar."

Caspar performed his deep salute, turned, drew the rose-pink curtains which emitted a sound of tinkling bells, and went out, his red slippers whispering on the paved floor, but becoming silent when they sank into the soft mink rugs....

CHAPTER THIRTEEN

I

A reunion dinner was held at the Savoy Babylon, arranged by Drake Roscoe on the night before the *Queen Elizabeth* sailed. The great dock strike had ended when Steve Mason's resignation was announced, and shipping conditions had reverted to normal. Although Tony McKeigh had spent a delirious hour with Viola that same afternoon (and had learned nothing concerning the Order of Our Lady which Roscoe didn't know already) he was awed by the beauty of Claudette.

"You know, Mark," he confided to Donovan, aside, "I wouldn't have believed there could be two such lovely girls in the world!"

Mark Donovan smiled, in his charmingly shy way.

"There's a third coming along! She's asleep just now. Roscoe has told me the whole story, and I needn't say you have my best wishes, and all my sympathy. I know from experience how hard it is to get anyone out of the clutches of Sumuru."

Tony thought of "the princess in the tower" (his own title for an imaginary story) and suppressed a groan.

He saw the party on board in the morning, as Drake Roscoe had other, urgent duties, and made the acquaintance of Claudette II. They had been allotted excellent accommodation, and a motherly stewardess who fell in love with Detty at first sight.

Detty, however, was not as happy as Claudette and Mark could have wished. She was always looking around for her "booful lady" and inquiring tearfully for "my Anna."

Mark had explained the situation to Tony. "You can see," he said, "how right we are to get her away from the influence of that damned witch! Detty's young enough to have forgotten all about it by the time we come back. And by that time, please God, Sumuru and all her gang will be where they belong!"

"Amen!"

And Tony McKeigh meant it—excluding Viola.

He went ashore shortly afterwards. His day was planned for him. He was enjoying his new job as assistant to a star Federal investigator, but had learned (which, indeed, he knew already) that Drake Roscoe could be something of a martinet.

Lingering, as he made his way along the decks of the huge ship, swept by a sudden nostalgia, by a wish that he, too, had been bound for England, he noticed a cream-coloured perambulator, with lace-bordered hood, built on the lines of a smart automobile, stationed on the promenade deck. He might not have noticed it at all, except that a very pretty nurse stood beside it.

As he glanced at her, she turned her head aside, swiftly adjusting a pair of sun-glasses.

There had been no implication in his glance. He recognized and admired beauty. But there was no room in his scheme of life now for anyone but Viola. He had forgotten the girl, his brain busy with more important things, before he went down the gangway.

In their state-room, Mark Donovan and Claudette were trying to explain to Detty that she could see the big ship just as soon as the stewards had stopped rushing about and all the visitors gone ashore. They were interrupted by their cabin steward. An important piece of baggage seemed to be missing, and as it was possible that the label had become detached, the steward asked Mark to go along to the square and see if he could identify it.

When Mark had gone, Claudette began unpacking, trying to keep Detty in a good humour by giving her odds and ends to put away. They were both quite busy when a page knocked, opened the door and asked:

"Mrs. Mark Donovan?"

"Yes."

"Will you please call at the purser's office right away. There's an important message for you."

Claudette hesitated, as the boy went out, then rang for the stewardess. She wasn't surprised when no one replied. She knew that at these times stewardesses have their hands full.

At last:

"Listen, darling," she said to Detty, "I shan't be gone two minutes. Go on putting things away until I come back. Promise you won't go out."

Detty nodded, absently. She was absorbed in stroking Claudette's mink coat, murmuring "booful lady" as she did so.

Claudette hurried out to the alleyway. She knew that sailing hour drew near, and was anxious to get the message in time. This "important message" worried her. She kept trying to imagine from whom it might have come and what it could be about.

She had not got further than the end of a long queue lined up before the purser's office when the door of the cabin she had just left was opened, and a very pretty nurse looked in. Detty gave her one glance, and then sprang into her arms.

"My Anna!" Tears rose to Detty's beautiful eyes. "My Anna!"

"Quiet, Detty!" Anna smiled, speaking in a whisper. "We have just time, darling, to see the booful lady before the ship starts."

"Booful lady!" Detty's tones were rapturous.

"Come along. You will have to be in a pram—"

"Won't go pram!"

"But you must, Detty, and keep very quiet, too, if you want to see her and be back in time. *Do* you want to see her?"

Detty did want to see her, desperately. She was quite conquered.

Just outside the door a cream-coloured perambulator was standing. Detty murmured, but submitted to being lifted in and covered up with a cream eiderdown overlay. Then Anna, whispering: "Not a sound, darling!" wheeled Detty along to a cross-alleyway, from there to an elevator, into which the man helped her to wheel the perambulator. Detty was taken down to a lower deck.

Anna, now, was so nervous that her hands, as they steered the perambulator, trembled wildly. She had put on dark glasses and was darting furtive glances right and left as they came to the gangway.

A sympathetic deck steward offered his services. "Takin' the kid ashore, Miss?"

"Yes. She has been allowed to see her mother off. But they said good-bye in the cabin. I have to take her home, now."

Anna's voice shook emotionally.

"Best way, poor kid." The steward glanced at Detty's wide-open eyes: little more of her was visible. "Picture, ain't she? Let me give you a hand. Here we are... I'll go first."

Detty found herself lifted on to the sloping gangway, and then, half-carried by the steward, down on to the dock. When they got there:

"Thank you so much," Anna said, and began to fumble in her purse.

"Thank *you,* Miss!" The steward pushed her purse aside. "It was a pleasure. When are her folks comin' back?"

"Next month."

"I'll be lookin' out for you!"

The steward ran back on board, and Anna was wheeling Detty towards the barrier, when a heavy hand fell on her shoulder.

"This time, Anna," came a snappy voice, "we really *have* got something on you!"

Anna turned, took one glance at Drake Roscoe and Kendal Coburn, and quietly collapsed on to the dock.

II

When Tony McKeigh was admitted by Miss Rorke to Apartment 365, high up in the Savoy Babylon Hotel, the woman detective smiled and said:

"Can you spare me for an hour, Mr. McKeigh?"

"I think I might."

"I needn't say don't leave till I get back."

She went out, closing the door.

Tony called: "May I come in?"

"I suppose so."

He found Viola sitting in the armchair by the window. An open book lay beside her—and an unfamiliar awkwardness overcame him.

"Mind if I sit down?"

"You can't very well stand for an hour. You are staying for an hour, I believe?"

He was longing to reply, "Not if I'm unwelcome," but didn't. In fact, he was beginning to discover, and dislike, certain aspects of his new job. He sat down.

"Don't pile it on too thick, Viola. This situation is none of my choosing. I will add, without prejudice, that I didn't choose the dope you slipped into my tobacco one evening,
either."

"I was obeying orders—and I suppose you are."

"Mine happen to correspond to my inclinations."

Viola lighted a cigarette, and watched smoke hanging motionless in the stagnant air.

"This atmosphere is choking me. Isn't it a sort of torture to deny open windows, even to a prisoner?"

"I agree it's a bit stuffy. But you get a certain amount of fresh air, don't you?"

Viola nodded.

"On the roof. And that strong-arm lady hangs on to me as if she thought I might try to jump over. Tell me, Tony, if I'm arrested, haven't I the right to ask to see my attorney? *Can* I be held like this? Is there any real authority for such a thing?"

Tony scratched his chin.

"That's put me out in one round! As you're a British subject, I imagine you're entitled to apply to your consul and claim advice. The phone's beside you. Call him up and see what he says."

Viola stared out of the window. It offered a wonderful prospect, for this wing of the Savoy Babylon towered high above its neighbours. Three aspirants to altitude records, one fairly near, the others more distant, were visible from there. She was watching one of the more distant buildings, one crowned with an ornamental cupola.

"You know I can't," she answered sadly.

Tony McKeigh filled his pipe, considered the pall of cigarette smoke, and put the pipe back in his pocket.

"Viola, dear, I know you can't, too. You see, Roscoe is really doing the decent thing. He has enough evidence to tie you in with Sumuru. And Sumuru is wanted for murder."

"So are a number of generals."

"That's *her* line of argument! But the point of immediate interest to you is this: You can be charged as an accessory and locked up in jail to-morrow, if Roscoe gives the word. Suppose he decided to write to your father?"

Viola turned to him swiftly.

"No! He couldn't, he wouldn't, do that! Drake Roscoe is a gentleman."

"Just as well for you," Tony told her, dryly. "Particularly in view of the fact that he doesn't regard 'Our Lady' as any kind of lady!"

"You mean, he won't write to Father?"

"I think I can promise you that. But unless the truth dawns, so to speak, and you recognize the facts of your position, I don't know that Roscoe, or anybody else, can save you from prosecution. Viola!" He jumped up, crossed, and knelt in front of her, holding both her hands. "Can't you see—can't you understand—that you have fallen into the power of a dangerous fanatic? I know what that power is like, so does Roscoe. I admit the woman's a perverted genius. But I could give you chapter and verse for *five* murders she has committed. You can't be serious when you say that *any* so-called vow can bind you to a cold-blooded assassin!"

Viola's blue eyes were very bright.

"It's just that you don't understand, Tony. There never was a revolution without bloodshed. And Our Lady is going to bring about a revolution. But she doesn't plan to wipe out thousands of mere dupes, as other revolutionaries have done. It is the instigators of misrule and the real oppressors of the people, who alone stand in her way."

Tony bent and held Viola's hands to his lips. He was beginning to despair. He lacked the art to find loopholes in the crazy logic of Sumuru. Her point of view (which something deep inside his mind, but something he couldn't express, told him was wrong, rotten at the core) seemed to be reasonable.

Viola believed in it, was prepared to risk her freedom, her life, for it. If she condoned murder, as evidently she did, what argument was left to him?

There was *one*. He hesitated to risk it. But at last:

"Viola"—he looked up at her— "what you say means that, very soon, we shall never see one another again. I couldn't bear that, if you could."

He stood up, bent over her, and held her through a kiss that seemed interminable.

"Could you bear it, darling?" he whispered, his face buried in the waves of her hair.

"There's no need for it."

Tony released her, and stood back.

"You mean—you're going to break with Sumuru?"

Viola forced a smile.

"I mean I'm going to tell you a lot of things I know you want to hear. Stop making love to me, and just listen. I'm going to try to make you understand why I serve Our Lady."

III

Our Lady was seated on the mink-covered divan. Under her gauzy dress, every line of her beautiful body seemed to quiver. Her hands gripped the edge of the divan as she bent slightly forward.

Philo stood before her, his head lowered. He wore his chauffeur's uniform. His powerful frame almost appeared to have shrunk. As he stood there, long arms hanging down in dejection, his pose suggested that of a tormented gorilla.

"Continue, Philo. My anger is not for you."

The golden voice was pitched in a low key.

"All went according to plan, My Lady." The man's barbarous accent became more than usually marked. "I drove little Frances Esterhazy to the apartment on East 57th Street where the other child was waiting. I left little Frances there and picked her up on my way back. The other child with Annette and the white perambulator, joined me, and I took them to the Cunard dock, and up to Mrs. Esterhazy's stateroom. Annette had no difficulty in getting on board. She was given a visitor's ticket."

"How long was the other child there? No one saw her?"

"No one. Her mother, for whom My Lady had booked a second class passage, came to Sister Frances' room soon after the child arrived and took her down to her own quarters according to plan."

"There were no witnesses of this?"

"None, My Lady."

"Continue."

"Sanchez removed a piece of baggage, unnoticed. As soon as Mr. Donovan came to look for it, the note was sent to his wife by a page."

"And she did as it directed?"

"Almost at once. Sister Annette wheeled the empty perambulator into the alleyway outside the Donovans' stateroom. She seems to have had no trouble to persuade the child to come with her. I saw them as Annette approached the gangway. A steward helped her to get the child down to the dock."

"And then—catastrophe!"

Sumuru sprang up, a wild thing. She raised her arms above her head, intertwined her fingers—then sank down on to the divan and sat there staring straight before her.

"And then, My Lady, it happened—there"—the deep voice vibrated with smothered fury— "under my own eyes. And I could do nothing."

"One of *my* women in the hands of the police..."

It was a soft whisper, yet it had a note almost of despair.

"Disaster, My Lady!"

"There is no such word in my dictionary, Philo! I'm sorry for Sister Annette."

Her inscrutable regard was raised for a moment to Philo.

"My Lady!" His deep voice shook. "She did her best. Her failure was no fault of her own!"

Sumuru continued to watch him.

"One life, even if blameless, must not be permitted to interfere with projects which concern so many."

Philo stifled a groan.

"My Lady—Silvestre, who is indispensable to us, would never forgive you! He is a Gascon. He might become a dangerous enemy."

Sumuru half closed her eyes.

"Yes—they are deeply attached. I had hoped for beautiful fruit from this union. I must consider the matter. Sister Frances has been prepared for a possible emergency—and she is shrewd, that one, a true Creole. Did they bring her ashore?"

"No My Lady. The ship was on the point of leaving, and the passenger concerned evidently had not been identified. But the F.B.I, man, Kendal Coburn, sailed with the ship."

"He may hold her at Cherbourg, or perhaps bring her back in the pilot boat. Leave me, Philo. I must think—I must think...."

IV

In the stateroom on the big ship where the impudent substitution had taken place, Mrs. Frances Esterhazy, a brilliant brunette whose beauty betrayed African traces, was going through a gruelling examination by Kendal Coburn. Mrs. Esterhazy was tastefully dressed, and perfectly poised. Coburn's tough face didn't seem to frighten her.

Mark Donovan was the only other person present. In their own cabin, Claudette knelt, clasping Detty (who couldn't make it all out), tears in her eyes and her lips moving in a silent, thankful prayer.

By Roscoe's orders, all disturbance had been avoided on the dock. Few passengers, if any, suspected that a kidnapping plot had been foiled.

"You say that your nurse's name is Eileen Maury, Mrs. Esterhazy? How long have you had her?"

"Less than two weeks. But she came to me highly recommended, and I found her absolutely trustworthy."

"Might I ask who recommended her?"

"Mrs. Alvarez, an old friend. Her husband is of the Brazilian embassy. But you begin to alarm me, sir. Is there anything wrong with Eileen?"

"That, I am trying to find out. Your little girl, whose name is—?"

"Frances, like my own."

"Your little girl came on board to see you off, in charge of Eileen Maury, who was to take her ashore. What then?"

"My car and chauffeur were waiting. Long ago they should be back in the hotel apartment."

"No doubt. I am rather curious, Mrs. Esterhazy, to learn why you didn't take your daughter with you."

"I shall be away less than a month. My husband, a French officer, has two weeks' leave. We hope to spend it together in Paris. He is meeting me at Cherbourg."

"He lived in France and you in America?"

"Not before!" Mrs. Esterhazy flashed a dazzling smile. "He was a military attache in Washington until recently. His recall alone separated us. But"—her expression changed— "you are frightening me. There has not been an accident to Eileen?"

Coburn glanced at Mark Donovan.

"I have no reason to suppose so. But, to set your mind at rest, I put a call through to your hotel some time ago. A reply should be here any minute."

Mrs. Esterhazy dropped into a rest-chair. She clutched the arms of the chair.

"Then you *do* fear something? Tell me! Tell me! This is torture!"

Mark Donovan, watching her, decided that Frances Esterhazy was a highly-talented actress, no doubt selected for that reason. Coburn's face remained grim.

"I have nothing to tell you. If—as I anticipate—the reply from the management reports all's well, your troubles will be over."

The reply from the management, taken by an operator standing by for that purpose, was brought in almost as Coburn spoke. He read it aloud:

"Mrs. Esterhazy's little daughter, Frances, now in apartment with Mrs. Esterhazy's maid. Brought back from Cunard dock by chauffeur, Ivan Benjamin. Interrogated, Benjamin reports that child ran to the car, alone. Nurse Maury missing."

Frances Esterhazy stifled a cry of joy. She fell back in the chair, covering her eyes with her hands.

"Sumuru's a genius!" Mark Donovan murmured. He raised his voice: "Mrs. Esterhazy—"

"Leave this to me!" Coburn warned. He pointed a finger at Mrs. Esterhazy. "I have been admiring your charming ankles. Forgive me. But I'm puzzled about that curious design tattooed on one of them. Most unusual, isn't it?"

The black eyes were uncovered. They blazed magnificently.

"You are very impertinent!"

"I have to be. You see, it's my business to find things out. So would you mind telling me, Mrs. Esterhazy, why you have that mark on your ankle?"

She stood up, turned her back on Coburn and walked to the open port, looking out.

"I was born in Haiti. My native nurse put that mark on my ankle when my parents were absent, to protect me from snake bite. My mother was furious. She tried to remove it. But nothing could remove it." She turned, defiantly. "Are you satisfied, Mr. Coburn?"

"More or less. You've been well covered, Mrs. Esterhazy. Nothing left to chance. Thanks for your help."

He nodded to Mark Donovan to go first, and they walked out of the cabin. In the alleyway:

"That woman is one of Sumuru's!" Mark began excitedly.

"I know she is."

"Aren't you going to hold her? She was the keystone of the whole plot to kidnap Detty!"

"I know she was."

"*Her* youngster (if it's really hers) never left the car—or never came in it. Her youngster was the alibi. Some *other* child was brought on board by Anna (now called Eileen), and that child must be on board right now!"

"I know she must. Probably down in the second class, where as likely as not there are fifty or sixty more. As neat a set-up as I ever saw! It worked either way—except for Anna!"

"But you're not going to let this woman go free?"

Coburn pulled up—they were walking along the alley-way—and grasped Donovan's arm.

"Listen! The way she's covered up, how can I take Mrs. Esterhazy? I shall advise Cherbourg, in case further evidence ties her in. But, as it stands, she's in the clear. I can't take a woman off the ship for having a snake tattooed on her ankle! The F.B.I.'s shackled with red tape, although you mightn't think it."

"But—"

"I know just how you feel, Mr. Donovan! But this thing has been figured out in such a way that the only one of the gang we're entitled to hold is Anna—now known as Eileen. I'm real sorry for Anna. She's as pretty as a cover-girl and, oh boy, was she taking big chances! I'd be glad to give her ten medals, but she'll maybe get ten years instead!"

CHAPTER FOURTEEN

I

Steve Mason's retirement from public life, on the grounds of ill health, had been hailed as a victory for law and order. Drake Roscoe looked upon it as a victory for Sumuru. He called at the Finelander Foundation Sanatorium shortly after the labour leader went there to recuperate. Although it seemed preposterous to doubt the probity of such a famous institution, this new association with the Finelander family struck a sinister note.

Miss Rhoda Finelander had not returned from Virginia, so that he had been unable to talk to her. But he believed (and Mark Donovan had agreed with him) that this wealthy spinster was an unconscious dupe of Sumuru—as many other prominent women had become in Europe.

Roscoe met the director, Dr. Richborough, whom he knew by repute for a physician of high standing, and was introduced to the matron, Mrs. Worley. It was quite impossible to doubt the integrity of either.

If any further plot against Mason was brewing, certainly they knew nothing about it.

"Miss Finelander," Dr. Richborough told him, smiling, "when she learned that Mr. Mason planned to come here, expressed some disapproval. But the articles of the Foundation are so explicit that we really had little choice."

"That's interesting," Roscoe murmured.

"Oh, Miss Finelander has marked opinions of her own, but she bows, invariably, to her late father's wishes. As it turned out, Mason proved to be an ideal patient. A typical case, Mr. Roscoe, of what's popularly called nervous breakdown. Concerning its cause, his memory is a complete blank. Very little to be done, except to keep him quiet and attend to his diet. Do you wish to see him?"

"Yes, if I may."

He was taken up to a sunny room with a prospect of part of the extensive gardens which surrounded the house. Steve Mason was sitting by the window, staring out. He turned lack-lustre eyes in Roscoe's direction as he came in. He gave no sign of recognition.

"Hullo, Mr. Mason! Feeling better?"

Steve Mason nodded.

"Fine."

"You will remember seeing me in Florida."

Mason shook his head. His mane of grey hair, Roscoe noted was now heavily streaked with white.

"Not at Fort Lauderdale?"

"Never been there."

"Oh, I must be mistaken, I suppose."

Steve Mason looked from Dr. Richborough to his visitor with a puzzled expression.

"Are you the specialist from New York?"

"No, I'm not. My name is Drake Roscoe."

Mason shook his head again, turned away and stared out of the window.

Dr. Richborough shrugged his shoulders and led Roscoe from the room.

"You see? That's his habitual condition. Pathetic, isn't it?"

"Very. Who's this New York specialist he's talking about?"

"The Austrian neurologist, Dr. Strausser, who has an office on Park Avenue. Miss Finelander recommended him to me for consultations some months ago. I called him in once and found him a first-class man. His knowledge of obscure forms of alienation seems to be remarkable."

"Indeed." Drake Roscoe began to think hard. "Is this consultation to take place to-day?"

"Oh, no. To-morrow. Poor Mr. Mason has no idea of times or dates, you know."

"I can see that, Dr. Richborough. At what time to-morrow do you expect Dr. Strausser?"

"At eleven in the forenoon. Do you want to meet him?"

"I believe I do," Drake Roscoe replied slowly. "Steve Mason's case interests me deeply."

II

But at about the same time, Tony McKeigh was studying another case, and one that interested *him* deeply.

If qualms of conscience troubled Tony from time to time, he smothered them under the consoling reflection that, after all he was doing exactly what Roscoe had instructed him to do! He was inducing Viola to talk.

She wasn't talking at the moment. They occupied the same chair, and Tony didn't seem disposed to stop kissing her until some later date. But at last, laughing breathlessly, Viola called a halt.

142

"I simply worship you," he declared hoarsely.

"You keep telling me so! But you won't give me even temporary ease of mind by telling me that you understand me. You know nearly all my history. You know how I came to realize that Our Lady is the last hope the world has of peace—of survival. You *will* harp on the few people she has been compelled to remove from her path. Why don't you feel like that about Viscount Montgomery or General MacArthur?"

And Tony could only remain silent.

"Our Lady's war is with the *other generals,* not with their wretched troops. When a Steve Mason calls out all the dockers, she doesn't send soldiers to shoot the dockers; she removes Steve Mason. If any of her people betray her, she treats them as any commander would treat a spy. One day—soon—if this blind government, or some other, equally blind, doesn't interfere, she will remove the danger which hangs over all the world. It won't cost a million lives. It will cost only the lives of those who are really responsible."

Tony McKeigh stood up, gently lifted Viola to her feet and replacing her in the rest-chair, he began to walk about, in unconscious imitation of Drake Roscoe.

His brain was in a state of chaos.

Allowing for the fact that he was hopelessly in love with Viola, he had to admit that she was keenly intelligent and highly educated. She had inherited fine British traditions. Yet—she was utterly devoted to Sumuru.

She seemed to be a comparatively new member of the "Order". (She told him that Sally Obershaw was the latest.) "Our Lady" had used her talents to the utmost, giving her desperately dangerous assignments to carry out. Viola was proud of this!

No soldier, decorated on the field of battle, could know a keener thrill than Viola knew when "Our Lady" told her she had done well.

This was bad enough. But what overwhelmed him was recognition of the fact that he could think of no valid argument to oppose these seemingly cold-blooded theories! They had all the colour of logic. Tony McKeigh knew in his bones that there was a fallacy somewhere—but he couldn't find it.

And then—Viola's soft arms were slipped around his neck from behind.

"Tony dear—I have told you all I know, all I believe. If only I can get you to see the truth, to forget the stupidity of a 'shooting war', I shall have helped you to understand why I serve Our Lady. Then ... it rests with you."

He turned, held her close. His eyes were fierce with longing.

"What do you mean, Viola? Make it clear."

"All you know you can tell Mr. Roscoe. If he takes me into court, I can tell no more. I can only suffer imprisonment. You may believe I deserve it. That's for you to decide. But—I love you, too, Tony. Do your best for me."

III

Less than an hour after Drake Roscoe left the Finelander Foundation Sanatorium, Dr. Richborough had a call from Dr. Strausser in New York.

"I am sincerely sorry, Dr. Richborough," came the sonorous voice, with its trace of accent, over the wire, "but I have to leave the city early tomorrow, and so my appointment to see Mr. Mason must be cancelled—unless, it would be possible for me to see him later to-day."

"If it wouldn't be troubling you too much, Dr. Strausser, I should welcome a consultation this afternoon."

"Good. Shall we say at four o'clock?"

"Mr. Mason will be ready to see you at four o'clock."

And at four o'clock Dr. Strausser arrived in his Cadillac, driven by his dark-faced chauffeur.

He was a man of distinguished appearance, of good figure, and correctly dressed. His greying hair, short moustache, small beard and gold-rimmed glasses, all belonged to the famous Viennese specialist. So did the courtly manner, the trace of accent.

In fact, even to one who knew the real man, it would have been difficult to recognize Ariosto.

"I have done my best to prepare the patient for your visit, Doctor. His state of apathy is what alarms me."

"It is not so uncommon, this apathy, Doctor."

"I agree—up to a point. But there are other symptoms which *are* uncommon."

"Tell me, please, of these other symptoms."

"They occur in his sleep, and are, of course, recorded by the night nurse. He frequently cries out 'Jane!' He says, over and over

144

again, that someone he calls 'that damned woman' killed Jane. I presume, Dr. Strausser, that the 'Jane' in question is Mrs. Charles Madderley, who was known to be his mistress."

"No doubt, no doubt."

"But—and this is serious—he also declares, at frequent intervals, that he will 'get' the person he calls 'that damned woman' if he dies for it! A marked suggestion, I feel, of incipient homicidal mania?"

"In this I agree with you. It is as you say, serious. Correct me if I am wrong, but I have heard that Mr. Mason is a heroin addict."

"That is correct."

"You have not deprived him, of course?"

"No. That would be a mistake at the present stage. He is due for an injection shortly." Dr. Richborough glanced at his watch. "Nurse Carter will be here in a moment for an issue."

As Dr. Richborough opened a cabinet and took out a small phial:

"You use the United States standard preparation, no doubt?" Dr. Strausser remarked.

"Yes." The phial was handed to him. "Why?"

"In Vienna, at one time—alas, no longer—we employed the German." Dr. Strausser walked across to a window, and adjusting his gold-rimmed glasses, seemed to be studying the label on the tube. "In my opinion, it was superior."

He came back, and returned the phial to Dr. Richborough. There was a knock on the office door, and an elderly nurse came in.

"This is Dr. Strausser, whom I believe you have met before Nurse Carter. When you have given the patient the injection we will come up for a talk with him."

"Very well, Doctor." Nurse Carter took the phial. "Shall I call down?"

"If you please, Nurse."

A few minutes later the call came, and the two physicians entered an elevator and went up to Steve Mason's room.

They found him sitting staring out of the open window, as Drake Roscoe had left him. He turned his head slowly as they came in and fixed his eyes, sunken under bushy brows, on the visiting consultant.

"This is Dr. Strausser from New York, Mr. Mason. He has come to see how you are getting on."

Steve Mason's gaze never moved from Dr. Strausser's face.

"Haven't I met you some place?" he asked listlessly.

"Not to my knowledge, Mr. Mason," Dr. Strausser assured him.

He went on to ask a number of purely medical questions, looked at the temperature chart, and listened to the patient's heart.

"Nearly through?" Steve Mason growled. "Because you're not finding anything out. How much does this visit set me back?"

When, after a few recommendations to Nurse Carter, Dr. Strausser retired and the two physicians were back in the elevator:

"What is your opinion, Dr. Strausser?" Dr. Richborough asked.

"There is a suppressed urge of some kind. A complex is here which it would take a long time and much patience to discover. It may not be pathological. Physically, the patient seems fit enough. You have made a complete cerebral examination, yes?"

"He won't submit to anything of the kind."

"H'm. Difficult. I should like to glance over what data you have Doctor, before I take my leave. I will submit my written report in the morning."

CHAPTER FIFTEEN

I

Sumuru was refreshing herself in the crystal bath, surrounded by rainbow fish, waving aquatic plants, and canopied by palms. In contrast with the pink coral from which the plants sprang, their varied shades of green, and the brilliant hues of the tropical fish, her bare body resembled a beam of white light as she glided gracefully from side to side of the pool.

Her hair entirely hidden by a gilded cap, an onlooker, had there been one (other than the negress Bella) could not have failed to suppose that he saw a vision of a water-nymph.

Swirling from point to point and scattering the painted fish as he went, the grey barracuda followed Sumuru untiringly. When she swam to one side of the crystal pool, he swept to meet her. When she crossed to the other side, the barracuda, with one lash of his powerful tail, shot around the impassable barrier which defied him, and was there to attack.

The baffled fury of this marine murderer seemed to increase. As Sumuru floated on the surface, laughing gleefully, the torpedo-like fish would retire into the obscurity of the outer pool. It was filled with sea-water, whilst that in the crystal bath was fresh.

But when, restored, she dived to the bottom, the grey shape materialized. Always, the barracuda was waiting for her, hungry jaws snapping angrily against this mysterious, invisible substance which held him from his prey.

At last, breathless, radiant, Sumuru swam to the ladder and mounted to a crystal ledge on which the Nubian girl stood holding a fleecy robe.

"Satan never tires of our sport, Bella!"

"One day, Madonna, he will kill himself by banging his silly head against the glass."

She wrapped her beautiful mistress in the fleece.

"That would be a pity. Satan would be hard to replace."

In an adjoining dressing-room, Bella, having dried Sumuru's body and massaged her all over with a preparation perfumed with *spikenard*, wrapped her in a mink-lined robe. Sumuru lay on a couch of ancient Egyptian pattern which had legs representing leopards' claws, whilst Bella began to brush her luxuriant hair.

"If someone asked you, Bella," she murmured drowsily, "to describe the colour of my hair, what would you say?"

"I could say nothing, My Lady. Only a great artist could describe it, in a painting."

"Great artists have tried. None succeeded. A great poet tried, too, in words"—she sighed— "he died. He had failed."

She was silent for a long time, soothed by the sensuous enjoyment of Bella's skill; but presently:

"Do you never long to return to the Nile, Bella? That was where I found you—up above Aswan."

"Often, My Lady."

"How old are you, now?"

"Sixteen, My Lady, I believe."

"You have learned many things, Bella, in the years between. You must have been nearly thirteen when I met you. Had you a lover? You have never told me."

"No, My Lady. But there was someone—"

"Of your own race?"

"Yes, My Lady. You think I am beautiful, for you have told me so. But *he*—"

Sumuru slightly raised the fringes of her dark lashes and glanced up.

"You interest me, Bella. Beauty must be perpetuated. Later to-night I will send for you. It is possible we might find this beautiful countryman of yours."

Faintly, a silvery bell sounded. Sumuru clapped her hands.

Draperies covering the door were parted, and Caspar bowed in the opening.

"You have news for me, Caspar?"

"Yes, My Lady. Ariosto is here."

"Has he failed again?"

"He did not inform me, My Lady. He is waiting in the saloon."

"I will see him here. Send him to me."

Caspar bowed lower yet, and retired.

Almost at once, Ariosto came in. He still wore the dress of Dr. Strausser, but had discarded the gold-rimmed spectacles and the short beard. He pulled up for a moment, glanced angrily at the Nubian girl, then came across, stooped, and kissed Sumuru's hands.

"I have something to report, Madonna. We should be alone."

Sumuru glanced up at Bella, smiling.

"Leave us, Bella. I will ring when you are to return."

Bella inclined her head, put away the brushes and went out. As the draperies fell behind her:

"Madonna!" Ariosto dropped to his knees beside Sumuru. "Twice, now, I have risked my liberty, my life, to serve you. Roscoe was at the Sanatorium this morning. He must have found out about the appointment for to-morrow."

"Therefore, you went to-day. That was wise."

"But it means—that he knows! 'Dr. Strausser' must disappear from New York!"

"Undoubtedly, my friend. I had foreseen this. But your usefulness in that capacity is ended, in any event, Only tell me that you have rid me of the pestilent creature, Mason."

"It is done, Madonna."

He bowed his head, rested it on the robed figure, and threw one arm over Sumuru. She lay still as if carved of stone.

"Control your emotion, Ariosto. You are trembling like an amorous mule. No doubt it was my recognition of the fact that men are driven by appetite and not by wisdom which led me to learn to despise them. You, my friend, hold degrees of three great universities. You have a good brain, and more than your share of knowledge. You are, in fact, clever enough to know that I am your mental superior—"

"Madonna! have I ever denied it?"

"Never. You are aware that I can plan like Machiavelli and execute like Napoleon. You are aware that I know more of certain sciences than you know yourself. Yet, the privilege of my conversation, the tones of my voice, which poets have extolled, the long hours of my society, you would barter gladly for the privilege of caressing my body for five minutes. You fool! You man-fool!" She laughed gaily. "If you are weary of Dolores, seek elsewhere, my friend. I am a repast vastly too delicate for your jaded palate."

"My Lady!"

"You have taken risks in my service, and you shall be rewarded. But the reward to which you presume to aspire is too high. You long to strip the robe from my body, to bruise my sensitive skin with coarse, sensual kisses." Sumuru laughed again, a

149

trilling of fairy bells. "Perhaps—one day—I shall permit you to exhaust your crazy passion in that sterile amusement. But the day must be of my choosing. Stand up. Talk to me sanely."

Ariosto's handsome face was pale, his hands were clenched; but he obeyed. When he spoke his voice was quite steady.

"The substitution was simple. Mason's night nurse gave the injection before I had entered his room. The symptoms should develop at midnight, not earlier."

"What facilities has he, Ariosto, for self-destruction?"

"He seems to be deprived of nothing. Homicidal mania is no more than suspected. There are his razor blades and other bathroom fittings. He is lodged on the sixth floor and below is stone paving. I recommended that all windows be left open at night."

Sumuru sighed and turned on the couch, so that for one moment, as her robe became disturbed, Ariosto had a glimpse of satin white curves. No dove-dancer in the world had anything to teach Our Lady of the art of subtle exposure. She wrapped the robe negligently about her and stood up.

"You have done your best, my friend. I am pleased with you. We must await a further report."

II

"I have a sort of notion," Drake Roscoe was saying savagely, "that you're talking clotted nonsense, Mac. This girl, Viola, is one of Sumuru's stars. That's clear enough. And she has done a first class job *on you!*"

"But, Roscoe—listen—"

"I'm tired of listening. It's your turn. What your story boils down to is this: Viola wants to go free in return for the information she has given you. I'm going to draw your attention to nine queries which had to be answered at the time I took over your valuable services." He crossed to his desk. "Here they are—"

"Wait a minute—"

"Listen. First query: Is Sumuru the Duchesse de Severac? Has Viola answered that one?"

"She says she doesn't know."

"I see. Second query: Is the woman who left in the *Ile de France* the real Duchesse? Anything on that?"

"Same as above. But, according to the French police, she is."

"No thanks to Viola for information! Query three: Has anyone called Viola Stayton disappeared from England?"

"You know the answer to that one. She's here with parent's consent."

"Queries four and five refer to Sally Obershaw. We know, now, that she joined voluntarily and is, or was, at the Chateau Garron. Query six: Is Rhoda Finelander a member?"

"Viola says she doesn't know."

"She doesn't seem to know much, does she? Query seven therefore remains unanswered also.... Query eight—Where is Sumuru's New York base?"

"Viola knows, but firmly declines to tell me."

"As I'm sure she has also declined to tell you why Sumuru has apparently taken an interest in you, that closes the list." He dropped the sheet of paper on his desk. "Apart from a lot of twisted philosophy which you seem to take damn seriously, you haven't learned enough from Miss Viola Stayton to fill your pipe!"

"Rebuke uncalled for, I thought."

"Oh, I admit you have done your best, Mac. My point is this: What has Viola told you that we didn't know already?"

"Not much, I admit, except that she has given me an insight into the workings of the Order which makes it easier to understand how recruits are picked up. Viola is only a junior, you might say, but she explains in a way that makes the thing look unanswerable. You have had an interview with Sumuru in person, and you admitted that she shook you."

"She did," Drake Roscoe confessed, staring hard at Tony McKeigh. "But she didn't manage to *convert* me!"

Tony began to fill his pipe.

"For that matter, Viola hasn't converted *me*. She has just made it infernally hard to let her go to jail—because she honestly believes she's working for the good of the world."

Drake Roscoe broke into one of his restless patrols.

"All fanatics believe in their own particular brand of reform!" he snapped. "That's what makes 'em so dangerous." He paused, turned. "Have you asked Viola if 'Our Lady' has ears like a faun—to quote your own definition?"

Tony started. "No, by God! I never thought of it."

"Mind seems to wander badly when you're with her! I think you told me that the lady who led you down to the ocean, in Lauderdale, wore a mink stole which concealed her ears?"

"Yes, she did. Although it wasn't until towards the last that I thought of looking."

"You see, this discovery of yours—if it *is* a discovery—gives us one valuable clue—a clue to something that can't be altered. This woman seems to possess extraordinary powers of mimicry, according to Scotland Yard. But she can't disguise her *ears* except temporarily!"

Tony put his pouch away, and lighted his pipe. Drake Roscoe went on pacing up and down in front of the desk.

"How about the other prisoner, Roscoe? I mean the official one, Anna—or whatever her real name may be."

"She has refused to say a word until she has communicated with her parents. I had forbidden harsh measures. It wasn't necessary, anyway. Coburn had done the same! Sumuru is the first would-be dictator in my experience to use beauty as beauty should be used!"

"It's part of her creed, Roscoe. She claims that the beauty of women can be made a lever to rock the world."

Drake Roscoe pulled up again, and fixed a penetrating stare on Tony.

"That's almost a direct quote from *Tears of Our Lady*! I can see you have been sticking close to your studies, Mac!"

Tony McKeigh knew that he had flushed. He knew that Viola's safety had become to him a matter of paramount importance. And he knew that he was beginning to sympathize with the objectives of the remarkable woman called Sumuru.

"I deserve that one, Roscoe! I'm crazy about Viola, and so—I'm not to be trusted any longer. I admit it."

Drake Roscoe crossed, grasped Tony's shoulder.

"Don't think I'm unsympathetic, Mac. But I have to know the facts. Because I have to figure the best way to use them. I'm working on that right at this present moment."

CHAPTER SIXTEEN

I

Detective-Officer Mary Rorke had left Apartment 365 near the top of the Savoy Babylon Hotel, locking the door behind her. She had gone to dinner.

Viola, seated in her favourite chair by the window, reading, waited for ten minutes. Then, closing her book, she went into the bedroom and came out carrying a beautifully fitted manicure case adorned with silver and enamel and the name of a Bond Street firm. She opened it, and adjusted a nail file between two harmless-looking studs attached to the lid. Next, she inserted a different kind of key in the silver lock and turned it gently.

A spot of red light appeared inside what looked like a bottle of nail varnish.

Then, taking a small torch from her purse, she switched off all the lamps, went to the window, glanced at her luminous wristwatch, and seeming to take a sight on some distant spot visible in the darkness, stepped back, pace by pace.

She flashed the light—three times, a pause—twice; then waited, watching.

Whatever she watched for didn't appear.

She repeated the signal.

And, this time, an answer came. From the top of a distant building, high up just under the cupola which crowned it, came three flashes, a pause, then two flashes.

Viola moved over to where the manicure set stood on a table. She spoke softly:

"Sister Viola reporting. Is Our Lady ready?"

"She has been informed," came the high sing-song of Caspar, clearly as though he had stood in the room. "Kindly wait, Sister Viola."

There followed an interval, silent, and then:

"Yes, child?"—in the golden tones of Sumuru. "Have you seduced him yet?"

"Almost, Madonna."

"You sound sad, Viola. You have not given too much too soon?"

"You know I could never do that, Madonna. I am sad because I have to do what you ordered me to do."

"Unless you mean that he has become distasteful to you I fail to understand. I believed—and I am rarely wrong—that you were happy to be with him. I should approve. That was why I threw you into his arms. There must be some unions of affinity, if we are to produce a perfect race."

"I love him, Madonna."

"That is good news, Viola. If you can win him to the truth this will be even better news. In the position he occupies (which I can improve) he will be invaluable to us. Why are you sad?"

Viola hesitated. She was biting her lip.

"I asked a question, child."

"Yes, dear Madonna! I should hate to think that Tony was weak enough to accept a creed in which he truly didn't believe—for *my* sake."

"You are troubled by strange scruples! How many men, now usefully enrolled in our Order, have been won to it by hunger for a woman? Re-study Chapter Ten of *Tears,* Viola. You will find—if you have forgotten—that it deals with desire as the force which rules the world. You should be proud to wield so great a power—the power of Helen of Troy—a power which belongs to women, alone."

"Yes, Madonna."

"Tell me—have you induced him to speak to Drake Roscoe?"

"I believe he has done so—to-day."

"If he is successful, I can deal with the rest. Sister Blanche is expecting you. Silvestre will be standing by. If he fails, you must resume seduction. Or—you can give him up. I should be disappointed."

"I won't—give him up, Madonna."

"I know that, Viola. You have proved your mettle too often to falter, now, in winning a man you want for yourself, as well as for the Order. Good night, child. Give Caspar the signal. I am always with you."

Viola turned the key in the silver lock and withdrew it. She replaced the nail file. Then, picking up the little flashlight, she stepped back three paces, and flashed the signal.

An answering signal came from under the distant cupola, and—

"Hullo, Miss Stayton," said a crisp voice. "All in the dark?"

Drake Roscoe stood just behind her in the lobby.

II

Viola's training served her well. She recovered poise almost at once.

"The light failed, Mr. Roscoe. I was looking for the phone. I'm afraid I didn't hear you come in."

"I shouldn't have crept in like a mouse, Miss Stayton. But apparently your doorbell had failed, as well! Let's see if they've put things right again." He flicked some switches. "Ah! all's well!"

As the room was flooded with sudden light:

"Hullo!" he went on, looking around, "I must have been mistaken. I could have sworn I heard you talking to somebody!"

Viola smiled, dropped back in the chair near the window.

"Perhaps you heard me cursing! I was just about to work on my nails, Mr. Roscoe, when the light failed."

She opened the manicure case, then glanced up and closed it again.

"Don't let me interrupt you."

"Please sit down, Mr. Roscoe. If you care to talk to me I'm quite ready to listen."

Drake Roscoe sat down, watching her. He was smiling. Viola was distractingly pretty, from her wavy hair down to her slim, dainty feet. Impossible to condemn Tony McKeigh for falling for a girl like this. Viola stood up and offered an open cigarette case, nearly full; a feminine thing inlaid with mother-o'-pearl.

He was about to take one. Then he changed his mind, shot a swift look at Viola's face.

"Thank you, Miss Stayton. But mostly I stick to cigars!"

Viola sat down again and lighted one of her own cigarettes composedly.

"It occurred to you they might be doped?" she said it as casually as though doped cigarettes were a commonplace "Well, they're not. I have pleaded guilty to all that I have done, and I admit that I drugged Mr. McKeigh's tobacco But it was a harmless drug."

"How did you know it was harmless?"

"Our Lady told me so. Our Lady never lies. I destroyed her photograph because she ordered me to destroy it—"

"Yes. That brings me to an interesting point," Roscoe interrupted. "What was there about that photograph which made her so anxious to suppress it?"

"I don't know," Viola answered quietly.

"Could it have been—I'm merely guessing—that it clearly showed one of her *ears?*"

Drake Roscoe, watching, saw that he had scored a hit. Viola flinched. In spite of her excellent self-control, he saw her start. Tony McKeigh was right. The lovely Sumuru had no lobes to her ears. It was a defect which would in no way detract from her beauty, a curious formation which only a physiognomist would be likely to notice.

And it hadn't been visible in the destroyed photograph; for it was not mentioned in the physiognomy chart appended by Scotland Yard.

Viola recovered herself in a flash.

"Why do you say one of her ears, Mr. Roscoe? Whatever can Our Lady's ears have to do with it?"

"Just an idea that occurred to me. Ears are a sure means of identification, you know. No doubt modern surgery can alter their shape, as it alters the shapes of noses, but ears are less easy to treat surgically."

"Is that so?" Viola forced a smile. "As you are here, Mr. Roscoe, perhaps you will allow me to ask *you* a question?"

"Go ahead."

"How long am I to stay confined in this apartment? You have no real evidence against me, so far as I know, to justify it. Except for the liberty I took in destroying a compromising photograph, there is only his own word to support a charge of drugging Mr. McKeigh. There was no robbery committed. The incident might be explained, if I cared to explain it, in an entirely different way."

Drake Roscoe watched her admiringly. His heart was warming to Viola Stayton. She was a game little fighter.

"I had come to a similar conclusion," he told her. "McKeigh has helped me, I must add. You have helped me, too ... I propose to set you free, Miss Stayton."

Viola stood up.

"Truly? You mean it?"

"Yes, I mean it. I'm asking McKeigh to take care of you, wherever you want to go. You can leave some time tomorrow...."

III

156

Drake Roscoe, having locked the door of 365, didn't return at once to his own, adjoining, apartment. He took the elevator down to the main floor. A police car, although in no way identified as one, always stood by outside. Roscoe got in, and was driven off.

It was late when he came back to the Savoy Babylon.

Tony McKeigh stood staring out of the window, apparently fascinated by the panorama of glittering Manhattan. He turned as Roscoe opened the door.

"Hullo, there! I began to think you had been making a tour of the night spots. In accordance with your esteemed instructions, I have stuck to my homework. You will find all data neatly filed and indexed on your desk."

"Good for you," Roscoe smiled grimly. "I have certainly toured some night spots, but not those you may have in mind. Sumuru hasn't been running quite true to form, and I'm taking a leaf out of her own book. The reporters were allowed to gorge themselves on Anna's one court appearance, so that all the United States is now familiar with Anna's charming face. Mrs. Esterhazy will be shadowed from the moment she steps ashore at Cherbourg."

"I wondered why you didn't bring Mrs. E. ashore here, right away."

Drake Roscoe lighted a cigar.

"That would have been running true to form—as I did by having Anna arrested."

"But what about the kid!"

"We could have got hold of the child and still let Anna slip away."

Tony McKeigh relighted his pipe, which had just gone out.

"It's quite possible," he remarked, "that without knowing it, I have become slightly nutty. Because the point of your last observation entirely escapes me. Why let Anna go?"

"For the same reason that a decoy duck is let go—to snare bigger ducks. But, at the time, I wasn't ready. To-morrow I shall be. You remember that bail was refused. But an attorney, who will say he is acting for Anna's parents, is making another application in the morning—and the court will grant it. A perfect convoy of detectives will surround Anna wherever she goes."

"You believe that, sooner or later, she'll go to Sumuru?"

"Or communicate with her—yes."

"And I believe she'll slip through your fingers—like Sally Obershaw and the Duchesse de Severac."

"She may. But she's more possible use at large than she is locked up. I have come to the same conclusion about Viola—"

"What! Really?"

"Really. Viola will be your pidgin, Mac. I have a hunch she won't run away from *you*! You must cling to her like a lion-hearted limpet! A flock of agents will be covering both of you. Make your own plans for keeping her in sight. Marry her, if you like."

"You seem to be inspired by a sense of urgency."

"I am!" Roscoe snapped. "The net's closing in on Sumuru. She made a mistake when she came here! I don't underestimate her—and I figure she knows and will run for it any day, now—Hullo!"

The phone buzzed. Roscoe took the call.

"Yes—Drake Roscoe here.... Oh—Dr. Richborough!... What's that? Your consultant arrived ahead of time. Yes, I have it all. Good God! Yes, you were right to notify me, Doctor."

When he hung up, Drake Roscoe turned a haggard look on Tony McKeigh.

"Steve Mason has just committed suicide. He threw himself out of the window soon after midnight—"

CHAPTER SEVENTEEN
I

"I suppose," Viola said drowsily, "I'm under what we call at home 'protective custody'?"

Tony McKeigh feasted his eyes on her. She looked radiant; and this was a radiant morning. The large, smooth-running car swept along Merritt Parkway with that effortless glide which only a first-class engine can produce.

"Hardly, Viola. I'm not a copper."

"I thought you were—or at least, a sort of special constable."

"That job is temporary! You're quite well aware of it."

Although he was perfectly sure that Viola knew just how matters stood, he couldn't overcome a guilty sense of hypocrisy. He knew, and no doubt she knew, that their driver was a police officer, that a radio car followed them. But the sense of guilt persisted. He began to see difficulties ahead. All the same, he was enjoying his assignment.

"Mrs. Edwards is expecting *me,*" Viola told him sweetly. "I required a rest, and fresh air—especially fresh air. So I called her. I know the line from 365 was wired, and so you're aware of this, I suppose. But she isn't expecting *you.*"

"Quite a nice surprise for Mrs. Edwards."

"But her cottage is very small."

"The weather's warm. I can sleep on the porch."

Viola glanced at him, and sighed.

"Do you seriously intend to follow me about for the rest of my life?"

"Seriously. You'll never shake me off again. Say the word, and we'll be married right away. Otherwise, your reputation is gone. Come to England with me. Roscoe can charge the trip to expenses, and I have long leave from my paper. He'd be delighted. Roscoe would stick at nothing to save you from a life of sin!"

Viola laughed. It was good to hear her laugh, although the madness of the situation, peculiarly mad even in a mad world, suddenly cast a chill upon Tony's high spirits, as though a sinister cloud had swept across the sun.

"You are talking nonsense, Tony. But—I'm glad to be with you.

And an operator at police headquarters was getting a message from the radio car following.

"Now in Connecticut. Leaving the parkway above Greenwich. Have contacted local police patrol...."

Viola was directing the driver. There are no roads more confusing than the roads of Connecticut. Half an hour later, they were speeding along beside what seemed to be the border of a large estate.

"Big place behind there, somewhere," Tony commented.

Viola nodded. "The Finelander property. One of the largest in this part of the state."

Finelander! Tony McKeigh experienced another chill. The name of that distinguished family—or of its last survivor-figured prominently in the *dossier* he had recently arranged for Drake Roscoe.

Steve Mason had died in the Finelander sanatorium. Rhoda Finelander was the owner of the hulk *John P. Faraway.* The Hispano used by the Duchesse de Severac had been traced to a Finelander garage.

And the shadowing car was reporting to headquarters:

"Now skirting Finelander property..."

II

Sister Annette (Anna, of the Donovan household), bail having been accepted from the attorney who applied for it, escaped reporters and went by taxi to the restaurant on the main floor of the Ironstone Building. She wore a smart suit which, with her other things, she had been allowed to collect from the hotel apartment of Mrs. Esterhazy. She looked, as she was, a very pretty girl very well dressed.

This scored a hit for Drake Roscoe.

The mysterious phone call from a certain office in the Ironstone Building to Anna at the Donovans' home he had had investigated. But the report suggested that it must have been made by someone using the line, but not employed by the League of International Fraternity to whom the office belonged. The inquiry had been carried out by Kendal Coburn, very tactfully, and he had come to the conclusion that the League could be ruled out as a suspect.

Roscoe had dismissed this clue as a false lead, until, quietly entering Viola Stayton's apartment, the night before her release,

160

because he could hear her voice as he passed her door, he saw a signal being flashed from a distant building—the Ironstone Building!

Viola didn't know that he had seen it. He had not told Tony McKeigh. But he had acted, without delay. The Ironstone Building was now infested with detectives.

As the result of a midnight conference at police headquarters, and numerous inquiries by phone, he had established contact with Silvanus Brough—the architect who had designed the Ironstone Building and supervised its construction in the early 'twenties. He counted it a stroke of luck that Silvanus Brough still lived in Manhattan, having occupied the same apartment on Madison Avenue for twenty-five years.

Brough himself answered the doorbell. He was a huge, hilarious man wearing evening clothes. He had a mass of white hair, thick, black eyebrows and the complexion of a ripe red apple. His grey eyes twinkled with repressed mirth as he stretched out a big hand. Silvanus Brough was altogether exaggerated.

"Step right in, sir!" he invited in a cheery bass voice.

"I was afraid I might be disturbing you."

"Disturbing me! Ho, ho, ho! The night's hardly begun, sir. I rarely turn in earlier than three."

They went into a room littered with trays of cigarette and cigar stubs, empty glasses, and the general atmosphere of a bar. In fact, there was a large bar at one end.

"Had a few friends stop in on their way to a party," Brough explained. "I have a different date, myself, later. Bourbon, rye, Scotch? Help yourself to cigars."

When the big man had settled down, facing Roscoe across a brimming Old Fashioned:

"As you come on Federal business," he remarked, "I suppose it's serious business. So fire away. Let's get it over."

"The business is very simple," Roscoe told him. "I'm interested in the construction of the Ironstone Building. As you designed it, no doubt you can help me."

Silvanus Brough said he could show him the plans, but Roscoe explained that he merely wanted to know the lay-out of the top floor. "What rooms, if any, are there right below the cupola, and what's inside the cupola—water tanks?"

"No sir. There's a tank on the floor below. It doesn't occupy all of it, naturally. What used to be the private offices of the late

Julius Ironside are up there, too. Now used, I believe, by the L.I.F.—the League of International Fraternity. Ho, ho, ho!"

"Quite a bona fide concern, I suppose?"

"Oh, quite, quite! It was founded by Lucy, old Julius's widow. Very pious woman. Has wealthy supporters—the Finelanders, the Delaboles and so on. When Lucy died, she left the whole floor to the League in perpetuity. Personally, I could never find out what the League was for!"

Drake Roscoe, now, was sure he could have told him but he didn't.

"I thought," Roscoe went on, "that I saw a light above the floor you mention—right up in the cupola. Is that possible?"

Silvanus Brough stared.

"When was this?"

"The other night."

"H'm." Brough carried both glasses to the bar and refilled them. "It might have been possible in old Julius's time," he declared, returning with fresh drinks. "But he's been dead for fifteen years."

"Why in his time?"

"Well—I'll tell you. Don't spread it though. But they're both gone, now, so it can do no harm. Old Julius was a great friend of mine. He was wealthy and hospitable, and as pious as his wife. At least, he acted that way. Built a big new church in his old home town. But he liked his little bit of amusement. Ho, ho, ho!"

Those happy memories made Mr. Brough laugh so heartily that he had to pause to wipe his eyes.

"When I had planned the building for the Ironstone Corporation, Julius said to me, 'Vane—what's going to be in that dome? There's room for two more floors.' I told him there would be two empty floors, with an outside stair clear to the top, of course. 'But the cupola is just a decoration, Julius,' I said. 'There'll be no windows!'"

"And are there no windows?"

"Some small ones on each level. But you can't see them. They're hidden in the filigree. Well—he studied over it, and at last he sprang his idea. Inside the cupola he had me plan a hideaway where he could have his bit of amusement! It was a little palace, sir, with a swimming-pool, if you'll believe it. I had to reinforce with four new girders to carry that swimming-pool."

"But the existence of this place surely leaked out?"

"Not in Julius's lifetime, sir! There's a private elevator from the street to Julius's offices. (The public elevators don't run after about eight o'clock.) And a very private staircase—inside a closet—to the cupola! I have seen some amusements up there, Mr. Roscoe, I assure you. Lucy found out when Julius died, and I had a lot of trouble with her. Poor Lucy! She wouldn't have a thing touched. Left it just the way it used to be, and walled up the staircase closet. If the good ladies of the L.I.F. knew what they had over 'em—"

"Then I must have been mistaken in thinking I saw a light up there?"

Silvanus Brough controlled his mirth for a moment.

"Possibly not, sir. Possibly not. It might have been old Julius's ghost, visiting the scene of his little bits of amusement! Ho, ho, ho!"

III

The phone on the long, narrow table lighted by an Egyptian lamp, buzzed faintly.

Our Lady, who wore her street suit, took the call.

"Madonna"—the voice seemed to be pitched low, cautiously— "Sister Annette is here."

"Sister *Annette?*"

"She is here at the League reception desk, Madonna."

"Is anyone else there?"

"No one."

"Take her through the President's office. I will have the door opened."

Our Lady hung up. Her wonderful eyes were widely opened, and their expression was almost one of fear. She touched a button beside her. Caspar came in silently.

"My Lady called?"

"Go down and open the door, Caspar. Sister Annette is here."

"Sister Annette, My Lady?" The perpetual smile seemed to be disturbed by a slight twitch. "But—"

"There are no 'buts,' Caspar. Bring her to me—and lock the door again."

"Yes, My Lady..."

More than ever like a sleepwalker, Caspar went out.

163

Sumuru was leaning forward, her chin resting in her upraised hands, when Caspar returned.

"Sister Annette is here, My Lady."

Caspar faded into shadows as Anna came impulsively towards the long table, her eyes brimming with tears.

"Madonna! How can I thank you—"

"Sit there, Annette, and look at me."

Anna dropped down on a cushioned stool set before the table, her adoring gaze never leaving the face of Sumuru.

"My Lady works miracles! When I was released this morning, I could hardly believe it. But Mr. Hepplewhite—"

"Who is Mr. Hepplewhite?"

"The attorney Madonna sent to offer bail for me!"

"I sent no one, child!"

"Madonna!"

"I had other plans. You have fallen into a trap, Annette! I am not angry. You had no choice. But I must think, I must think."

Anna clasped her hands, desperately.

"Madonna! What has happened?" she whispered.

"Be silent, child. I must think."

Although Anna hadn't seen Our Lady call him, Caspar appeared like a ghost.

"Yes, My Lady?"

"This brief visit to our New York headquarters is over, Caspar. There will be sacrifices, but we must leave at once. Sister Julia, at the League reception desk, is safe. She can remain. Nothing can be proved against her. The other members of the staff are not ours."

"My Lady! This is an emergency?"

"An emergency, Caspar. Where is Philo?"

"With the big car, My Lady. It is parked near the private entrance."

"Instruct Philo to proceed, immediately, to the Savoy Babylon and to call The League from there."

"Yes, My Lady."

"Sanchez?"

"He is free until six. But I could leave orders for him."

"Leave an order that he is to take the Cadillac, drive it to the garage and await orders. Who is on duty to-night?"

"Sister Berenice."

"Instruct her not to come. She is to await further orders. Ariosto is due. He must remain, for the present. So must you. Instruct Silvestre—"

"My Lady—Silvestre has other orders! He may already have carried them out—"

"True! I had forgotten! That exit is closed."

But no trace of emotion disturbed the golden voice, nor marred the serenity of a lovely face.

"I could call him, My Lady! It is just possible—"

"No. Let *that* trivial detail, at least be successful. My failures, in this barbarous city, outnumber my successes. I have relieved them of the man, Mason—a lesson to would-be dictators of industry. The little Claudette, a wonder-child, is lost to the Order. And two of my women have betrayed me—"

"Madonna!" Anna whispered, fearfully.

"Not you, Annette. You did all that I asked of you." Sumuru turned to Caspar, who stood, head lowered, listening. "Sister Bella is on duty. Bring her to me here."

Caspar *salaamed* and went out. Anna sat silent, watching Sumuru.

"It may be as well, Annette," Our Lady went on, musingly, "that this has happened. Drake Roscoe released Viola to-day. He must have other evidence. We have little time."

Caspar returned, as quietly as he had gone. The shapely Nubian came with him. She wore a white, nurse's dress, and stood immobile as a statue, awaiting orders.

"Stand up, Annette." Anna stood up. "Stand beside Bella."

The two beautiful girls, unlike except for their shapely bodies, stood side by side.

"Look Caspar! There is no more than a shade of difference in their heights. You were formerly used to smuggling human contraband. Since those days, you have added to your experience in my service. Sister Bella is your model, Sister Annette your canvas. Work fast."

Anna and Bella looked at one another, uncomprehendingly. But:

"It will be difficult, My Lady," Caspar declared. "But I will do my best." He glanced at the two girls. "Be good enough to follow me."

165

CHAPTER EIGHTEEN

I

A woman F.B.I. agent, hand-picked by Drake Roscoe, was interviewing the receptionist in the offices of the League of International Fraternity. The receptionist, handsome, grey-haired, having charming manners, seemed anxious to answer her inquiries.

"I am so interested in these poor Albanians," the visitor explained, "and I know your League has helped many unhappy exiles. Could I see the president, do you think?"

"The president, unfortunately, is not here. The vice-president might be able to see you. But I'm afraid you would have to make an appointment. She only comes up for a few hours, in the morning, and left ten minutes ago. Our secretary, Mrs. Carmichael, could probably give you more information."

"Thank you. I should be glad to see her, if she's disengaged."

Sister Julia took up the phone. While she was waiting, a pretty coloured girl with superb figure and carriage, came from the inner office and walked out to the elevators.

"What a beautiful girl," the visitor remarked.

"Yes," the receptionist smiled. "She comes from somewhere up the Nile, I believe. We were fortunate enough to place her in a good position. She often stops in to see her sister, who is employed here."

But Anna, not yet confident of the success of Caspar's cunning transformation, hardly dared to breathe until she was in a taxi bound for the real Bella's apartment, of which she had the key. Her own suitcase was to be sent on, and her orders were to take the midnight train to Alabama. "A place will be reserved for you by the League," Our Lady had told her, "in the name of Belle Davis. You will receive instructions by phone, later, where to leave the train..."

Anyone boarding an elevator on the floor occupied by the League was being shadowed to his or her destination. A plainclothes man travelled up and down in every car for this purpose. The unobtrusive door on the street which belonged to the private elevator was covered. But no one came out that way.

In fact, after Anna came down, no one else left the League offices except callers (all of whom were shadowed) until the staff left at five o'clock—a cosmopolitan collection which included the real Bella.

The report on Anna suggested that she was a bona fide protegee of the League (as Sister Julia, the receptionist, had told the woman agent). Discreet inquiries at the apartment house where she lived, and to which she had been tailed, resulted in the information that Belle Davis was a good, quiet and highly respectable tenant, lived alone, and was employed as nursemaid by a well-to-do family who often took her away with them to look after their two children.

When the L.I.F. offices were finally closed for the day, and Anna, who had certainly gone in, apparently hadn't come out, Drake Roscoe smiled grimly at Kendal Coburn.

"She's jumping her bail! But we'll catch her upstairs!"

It was a natural deduction. But he was dealing with a supernatural illusionist.

II

The way to Mrs. Edwards' cottage was up a long, narrow, winding lane, screened by old trees. The cottage, as Tony McKeigh saw, had begun life as a log cabin, but had been enlarged and modernized. It stood in a three-acre clearing, all cultivated and well-kept.

Mrs. Edwards came out from the porch to meet them.

Early middle-aged, she was of the Scandinavian type, blonde with fair skin and a tall, shapely figure. It was a type very popular in show business, and Tony wondered if Mrs. Edwards could be an ex-chorine. That she was a member of the Order he took for granted.

He could detect no sound to indicate that the police car following had entered the narrow lane.

"Good to stretch my legs," he sighed, as he got out.

Mrs. Edwards welcomed Viola smilingly, and Viola, turning to Tony, said:

"This is Mr. McKeigh. He has insisted on coming with me but I don't know what we're going to do about him."

Tony shook hands with the tall blonde woman.

"Where's the nearest magistrate?" he asked.

"Magistrate?" Mrs. Edwards glanced sharply at Viola.

"We want to get married, you see, Mrs. Edwards. Viola doesn't like the idea of living in sin."

And even Viola's admirable poise couldn't disguise the flush which coloured her cheeks.

"Please pay no attention, whatever, to anything *hi* says! Can you possibly find room for him, somewhere, Mrs. Edwards? It's hopeless to try to shake him off."

Mrs. Edwards murmured something about the woodshed, but her smile was reassuring.

"I know what *you* would like after your drive," she said affectionately taking Viola's arm. "A cup of real English tea."

"Yes, I would. Probably, you"—Viola turned to Tony—"would prefer a glass of real Scotch whisky?"

"Not at all. You must avoid jumping to conclusions, darling, if our life together is to be a happy one. Mine is tea, definitely."

The police chauffeur was taking out two suitcases. He exchanged a significant glance with Tony McKeigh.

"You needn't wait, driver," Tony told him. "I'll call the garage when I want you."

But as he walked in behind Viola and Mrs. Edwards he was wondering what the man's real instructions had been. He was wondering, too, how this rather embarrassing situation was going to resolve itself. And he was wondering what had become of the police car.

In fact, the police car, with one man left in charge, had pulled up at the entrance to the lane, where a notice announced that there was no way through. The rest of the party had followed on foot. Their orders were explicit. Drake Roscoe still remained uncertain concerning the whereabouts of Sumuru. She might be in Manhattan, undoubtedly her headquarters, or she might be in Connecticut, where she had powerful supporters.

"Who is this Squadron-Leader Silvestre?" Tony McKeigh was inquiring, suspiciously, as he lighted a cigarette. "And why does he want to meet me?"

His cup of real English tea had made him feel pleasantly drowsy.

"He is Miss Finelander's pilot. She has two private planes," Viola told him. "And a landing ground quite near by. Her small plane came in this morning from Virginia."

Tony McKeigh tried to remember Roscoe's instructions. At last:

"Is that so?" he said. "Then I'm fully in favour of taking a look at same."

He and Viola started out, whilst Mrs. Edwards cleared the cups away. Their route led from the back of the cottage, through a woodland path, cool and deep in shadow. Ten paces along, Tony paused.

"Darling!" He took Viola in his arms. "It wasn't a joke—what I said to Mrs. Edwards. I meant it. Viola—you *will,* won't you? I know Mrs. Edwards is one of the gang, and I suspect that the Finelander woman is another. I know you're one, too. But I don't care! I'm not a blind fool. My eyes are wide open when I tell you that I'd sign on with Satan himself for *you!"*

She trembled as he kissed her, but returned his kisses, wildly. The woods around were still.

"Say yes!" It was a breathless whisper in Viola's ear.

"Yes, Tony, dear! And now, let's hurry along—"

But it was some time before they came out of the wood—and faced a large expanse of level meadowland on which an L-shaped landing-strip had been laid out. On one runway, facing south, was a small greyish plane, an unusual model. It reminded Tony McKeigh of a resting locust. At the moment that he and Viola left the woodland path, a smartly dressed pilot came to meet them. He wore a black Musketeer moustache, beneath which his teeth glittered when he smiled, and his salute was a perfect Gallic gesture.

As the gallant Frenchman stooped to kiss Viola's hand, Tony McKeigh experienced the first pang of jealousy ever to trouble a carefree life.

"This is Squadron-Leader Silvestre," Viola was saying. "Mr. McKeigh."

"A pleasure to meet you, Captain McKeigh," the handsome pilot declared, gripping Tony's hand. "We served in the East together but never chanced to come together. I am glad to have the privilege of showing you one of England's finest ships. Only three models exist. A Carradale Sniper Hornet."

Squadron-Leader Silvestre spoke perfect English, yet, for some reason, the meaning of his words seemed to escape Tony. It appeared to him, also, that the Squadron-Leader's butter fly moustache was increasing in size.

The Police Captain who led the covering party, with one assistant crept cautiously through undergrowth and lay watching the meeting. The other two members had been thrown out on the flanks and were making their way under cover cautiously to draw up level with the plane.

"What do we do now, Captain? Grab 'em?"

"Got no orders to that effect."

"But look! They're going aboard! Seems to me the Englishman's drunk. Hi! what's this..."

It was a scene of sudden activity, in which other figures, coming out of a hut near the runway, joined. It was a scene which led to a wild blast from Police Captain Ford's whistle; to a rush from cover of the two detectives on the flanks.

And all too late...

Tony McKeigh had a vague impression of a roaring sound, as though a million-ton shell had passed by. He had no other impression whatever until he found himself in Viola's arms, her tears wetting his cheeks and her kisses on his lips.

"Tony, darling, forgive me! You *must* forgive me ..."

He tried to close his eyes. But his eyes wouldn't close. This was a dream. He must wake up. He had dreamed that Viola lay in his arms, crying.

His eyes remained wide open—and the dream was no dream. It was true. He tried to get to his feet—but he couldn't move. Viola clung to him.

"I'm a desperate little hypocrite—but don't hate me! don't hate me! I love you. You won't be able to move for a few minutes. It's *ahbowanee.* It's harmless. It was in your tea... You frightened me in the wood. I thought I should never get you to the plane. There was no other way."

He was fully conscious, now. But not a muscle of his body responded!

Then he remembered that Drake Roscoe had had a similar experience. He tried speech.

"Viola!" (He could speak!) "I believe I like being kidnapped! Is Silvestre the pilot?"

"Yes, Tony."

"Why does he work for this damned woman?"

171

"Sister Annette's his wife. You know her as Anna. She was nurse to the Donovan baby. Jean Silvestre adores her. She's the daughter of an Irish baronet and a perfectly sweet girl."

"I'm sure she is! All sweet girls go in for baby-snatching. Silvestre must look forward to seeing her when she comes out of jail?"

"He trusts Our Lady."

"Nice for him. Might I inquire where we land?"

"The Azores. There may not be time to get married there—but I'm all yours, darling..."

CHAPTER NINETEEN

I

"Everybody who came out of those offices," Coburn assured Drake Roscoe, "was checked and covered."

"Sure nobody walked down the stair and joined an elevator on the floor below?"

"Dead sure. Two men were posted at the foot of the stair. Nobody came down."

"Did anyone, as well as Anna, go in, who *didn't* come out?"

"Yes. One is reported."

"Who was it?"

"From her description, a daily worker who cleans the offices after the staff has quit. She went in just before Mrs. Carmichael—who's the League secretary—came away."

"So she's in there now?"

"Must be."

Drake Roscoe looked haggard with worry. Some hours before, he had received the news of Viola's escape, taking McKeigh with her. And he had an uneasy suspicion that Sumuru might be on that plane. The crestfallen party in Connecticut wanted to make arrests. Roscoe knew that no charge could be laid against anyone concerned. The plane was properly licensed and, even if he had known its route, he had no authority to attempt to intercept it.

He was fighting with shadows—and he was fighting mad.

"This woman will probably be done soon. We might ask her some questions when she comes out. But I don't want to start anything until all the offices in the building are empty. If it once gets around that a raid's pending, we shall have a damn great audience."

But at eight o'clock, when the elevators normally closed down, the office cleaner hadn't reappeared.

Some twenty uniformed police and a dozen agents alone occupied the Ironstone Building...

II

"You have the address, My Lady?"

"I have it, Caspar. Instruct Philo to meet us at a convenient point."

"Yes, My Lady. Patrolmen are entering the building singly and in pairs. I have counted eighteen."

My Lady's level brows were drawn down in reflection.

"Are all these men from the same precinct, Caspar?"

"No, My Lady. It seems to be a selected party picked for special duty. There are a number of plainclothes operatives, who may be police detectives or F.B.I."

"Drake Roscoe?"

"Must be somewhere inside. I have not seen him recently."

"Notify me of any fresh development."

"Yes, My Lady."

Caspar's voice ceased. The little green light on the cabinet went out. Sumuru stood up.

And on the other side of the street, nearly opposite the entrance to the Ironstone Building, a slightly built taxi-driver returned to the job (whatever it was) which had kept him busy, hood raised, spanner in hand, for the past hour. His was an elderly, yellow taxi, so that its breaking-down didn't seem surprising. The ivory face of the driver wore a patient, never-changing smile.

The vicinity of the Ironstone Building becomes oddly deserted after business hours, and the few passers-by weren't interested in the stranded taxi....

Sumuru began to walk from room to room. A delicately appointed bedroom she went into, first. It was fragrant and lavender-scented, totally out of keeping with the exotic apartments which surrounded it. Only the dresser showed wild disorder. She opened the door of a deep, wide closet, and sighed.

It contained dozens of the most perfect mink coats, cloaks, wraps and stoles, many of them unique of their kind. They ranged from snow-white to deep, shimmering brown, almost black.

Our Lady caressed them lovingly, sighed again, and closed the door.

She walked through the dressing-room with its Egyptian leopard-legged couch and out on to the crystal ledge above the swimming-pool.

Sumuru looked down into clear depths.

As though her mere reflection had animated the tireless killer, there came a swirl in the outer tank. Aquatic plants swayed as if swept by a sudden current. Brilliant tropical fish scattered like living confetti. And out of shadows the barracuda shot, torpedo fashion, towards the taunting image.

Our Lady laughed gleefully—the laughter of a child, of a nymph flying from a faun; silver laughter filled with the music of magic.

"Good-bye, Satan! Good hunting..."

She turned away reluctantly and went out through the dressing-room, and up a narrow staircase. She opened a silent, sliding door and stood in the domed blue pavilion lighted by mosque lamps and heavy with the heady perfume of mimosa.

A patrolman was seated on the ledge of the pond, looking down through leaves of water lilies at the red fish gliding below.

Slight though the sound Sumuru's entrance had made, the patrolman looked up quickly.

He was Ariosto.

As his glance swept over Sumuru, a look of mixed horror and despair crossed his face.

"Madonna!"

The word was almost a groan.

"I see that you approve of me, my friend! Am I not a great artist?"

"Madonna!" He buried his face in his hands. "None of this was necessary. We could have left with the others, and be in safety, now—"

"Your love of danger, Ariosto," she taunted him, "is deserting you. Am I to fly under cover of my servants and my slaves? I have a first-class brain, Ariosto, but I am a woman. This means that some petty triumphs seem more worth while to me than great conquests."

She crossed and stood beside him, looking down into the pond. Except for the tinkling of the fountain, there was no sound, until:

"I hope they will know how to tend my golden orfe," the lovely voice murmured.

III

Deputy-Commissioner Reardon had joined the raiding party. His presence was unnecessary, but unavoidable. He stood beside Drake Roscoe on the staircase, facing an iron door which barred the way to the floors up in the cupola.

It carried a notice, printed in red, which said:

"*This door to be kept locked. By order of the* Fire Department."

"You see," Roscoe was saying savagely, "this door wants a bit of shifting! What does that notice mean? Don't regulations provide for an outside stair clear up to the top?"

"H'm!" The Deputy-Commissioner removed his cigar and looked at the lighted end as though it surprised him. "Maybe dates back to Julius Ironstone's time. Doesn't look new."

"But Julius Ironstone was bound by the same regulations as anybody else."

"M'yes. Except that Julius Ironstone had more money than nearly anybody else," was the cryptic reply. "Where do we go from here, Mr. Roscoe?"

"Through to the League offices. We have all the other keys—but no key for that door."

They went through to the outer office. A party under Coburn had searched every square inch of the place with the exception of a large closet in the general office and the door marked "President" which none of the keys in the bunch surrendered by Mrs. Carmichael would open.

"Shall we smash them down?" one of the men wanted to know.

"No." Roscoe was peremptory. "No damage, unless we're forced to it. We have nothing on the League of International Fraternity, as such. The people we're after are on the floor above."

He crossed to the door of the President's office and tried it.

"Sure there's no key?"

"Certain," Coburn assured him. "The one marked 'President' doesn't fit, and we have tried every other Yale on the ring."

Police and agents were crowding behind him, when:

"Quiet!" Roscoe snapped. "Listen!"

He had his ear to the panels of the door. But not only he, but many near by, heard what he had heard... *a faint moan*!

"That settles that!" The Deputy-Commissioner dropped his cigar on the parquet floor and put his heel on it. "Who's the best man at smashing doors?"

This inquiry produced a chorus of volunteers. Everyone deserted the general office and hurried to reinforce the excited group surrounding the door marked "President." So that when another locked door (that of the closet) was quietly opened and a patrolman stepped out, no one was there to see him.

Relocking the closet behind him, Ariosto mingled with the others.

A crowbar was passed forward, and a man went to work scientifically on the job. It didn't take long. In a matter of three minutes or less the door was wrenched free of its hinges and forced open.

The office inside showed black as a cavern.

"Lights!"

Half a dozen lamps flashed to life. Then, the switches were found and the President's office became brightly illuminated.

Behind a large, empty, shiny desk a woman sat gagged, bound to a heavy chair!

The most prominent feature of her face visible was a closed and discoloured eye, the other eye glared at them madly. Dusty-looking grey hair hung down like a dirty mantilla over nearly purple features glistening with perspiration. She wore a shapeless blouse, an old brown skirt, felt slippers and rubber gloves.

On a hook in one corner of the office, a black hat, a plaid topcoat and a large bag were hanging. On the floor below stood a pair of shoes. Near by, a carpet sweeper and a mop were propped against the wall near a bucket.

They got the gag out first. It was a large cork secured to a piece of lint tied firmly around the woman's head. It was so tightly wedged between her yellow teeth that evidently she had tried to bite through it. Then, willing hands cut the lashings which bound her wrists and ankles.

Drake Roscoe helped her to her feet.

"Hould me up," she moaned. "Me feet is dead."

She was supported to a couch in the reception office. She collapsed there, but declined medical aid.

"Get me a drop o' whisky and then put me in a cab. Sure, me ould man'll be tearin' the Bronx apart!"

She was Mrs. Murphy.... "Fifteen years come Michaelmas I've done these offices, and never the likes o' this has happened to me."

It was her custom, she told them, in such a broad brogue that it was difficult to understand her, to begin her work in the President's office. She was in there, and Mrs. Carmichael had only just left, when the lights went out and someone attacked her in the dark.

"Oi think of passed out entoirely. I woke up the way ye found me..."

A sympathetic Irish policeman brought her hat, topcoat, bag and shoes and escorted her down in the one elevator still operating. An elderly yellow taxi appeared just when it was wanted and Mrs. Murphy gave an address in the Bronx.

Officer Rooney's sympathy went so far that he forced a dollar bill on her, towards the fare. "Wid me best wishes, Mrs. Murphy. Sure, it's a game ould soul ye are, and it's Mike Rooney that says it!"

CHAPTER TWENTY

I

"THE door to the private stair is somewhere in this room," Roscoe declared. "And we're going to find it." He turned to the Deputy-Commissioner. "Plain enough what happened. Mrs. Murphy must have been in the way to-night. She had to be silenced—"

He stopped, suddenly. His expression changed.

"*Why* was she in the way?" he went on. "Because *somebody* wanted to come out!"

"Maybe *did* come out," Coburn suggested. "That closet in the main office—"

"Smash it open!"

Men ran to carry out the order.

"If you say there's a hidden door in this office, Mr. Roscoe," the Deputy-Commissioner said, "we must strip the panelling off if necessary and find it."

The work of destruction began. There is nothing any search party enjoys more than smashing other people's property.

First to go was the closet in the main office. The searchers had a Mother Hubbard reward. Apart from stationery, files, and other equipment, "the cupboard was bare." But it provided ample accommodation for anyone in hiding.

"Strip those shelves. Sound all the walls...."

Then came a call from the President's room:

"Here's the door, sir!"

Drake Roscoe ran in.

A section of the panelling had been torn down. Part of it had been attached to the hidden door.

"Which proves," Roscoe snapped, "that the panels covering the door open with it. There's some simple mechanism some-where."

He began to study the area covered by the door.

"As it's sure to be fastened from the other side, sir," a voice came, "we might as well go to work to break—"

The man stopped speaking. There was a decorative wall-lamp on the panelling. Drake Roscoe pulled the chain to light it— and the whole panelled section swung open!

"As neat as anything I ever saw!" Coburn declared.

There was a carpeted stair inside. Roscoe turned in the opening.

"I want everyone else to stand by down here. Mr. Reardon—Coburn—come with me."

The three investigators, Roscoe leading, started cautiously to go up. There were no lights on the stair, but they could see light above. It came through the chink of another door on the upper landing.

"Be ready for anything!"

Roscoe pushed the door wide open.

They stood in a lobby, dimly illuminated. It contained no furniture; but their feet seemed to sink into the soft floor covering. Coburn shone a light downward.

"Great snakes! Mr. Roscoe, look at this!"

Drake Roscoe looked.

The lobby was carpeted with mink fur.

There was no sound.

They went ahead, came to a tiled pantry and to a small but perfectly equipped kitchen. Beyond was a tiled corridor. Mink rugs were on the floor. It led, one way, to the lavender-scented bedroom, the other, to the small library with its long, narrow desk on which an Egyptian lamp was still alight. Nothing stirred anywhere.

Roscoe, angry despair clutching him, stood looking at the objects on the long table when a cry came from Deputy-Commissioner Reardon. Roscoe and Coburn joined him at a run.

He had found the dressing-room, the Egyptian couch, and exploring further, stood now on a narrow crystal ledge pointing down into the tropical pool.

"God's mercy! There's a great barracuda down there! What's this place for? No one dare swim in it."

Drake Roscoe caught his breath, stared hard, and solved the mystery.

"Safe enough. It's a double bath. Those things are swimming outside it."

There followed some moments of silence, and then:

"Mr. Roscoe"—Reardon spoke in a hushed voice— "this woman Sumuru, if there really is such a person, must in the first place squander millions of dollars, and in the second place be raving mad!"

"What I want to know," Coburn broke in, "is this: Where *is* she?"

Reardon opened the door of the big fur closet and gave a gasp of amazement.

"Will you look at *this!* No one woman in the world ever owned all this mink before!"

But when they discovered the second stair, and found themselves in the blue-domed pavilion, their stupefaction became complete.

"To think," the Deputy-Commissioner muttered, "that I'm not dreaming. That I'm on the top of the Ironstone Building! There were rumours about Julius Ironstone back in my college days, but I'll swear even Julius never fitted out *this* place!"

"Do you know the lines of Coleridge, 'In Xanadu did Kubla Khan a stately pleasure dome decree'?"

"I'm afraid they're new to me."

"They were evidently not new to Sumuru."

"Listen!"

The word came from Kendal Coburn. He was standing near one of the arabesqued walls. Silence fell, except for tinkling of the little fountain.

A stifled moan became audible.

Coburn began groping with the beautifully inlaid panels, and presently a sliding door quietly responded to his efforts.

Inside a small cabinet, solely furnished with a cushioned divan and a lighted hanging lamp, they found an elderly woman, very scantily clothed, who seemed to be just recovering consciousness.

Like a thunderclap in the brain, the truth burst on Drake Roscoe. He clenched his fists and clenched his teeth.

They managed to restore her.

She was Mrs. Murphy, the office-cleaner.

II

Those fabulous rooms in the cupola of the Ironstone Building were gone over in scrupulous detail. Sufficient data was discovered to open many lines of inquiry, but no positive evidence incriminating anybody.

Drake Roscoe sat alone at the long, narrow table, studying such documents as he found there in the light of the one Egyptian lamp, when the phone at his elbow buzzed.

181

He started, then took the call.

"Hullo."

"Ah, Mr. Roscoe! I was hoping I should find you there," came the unforgettable golden voice. "It's rather a stalemate, isn't it? But at least you have driven me out of Manhattan. I wish you had given me time to see you again. But I have to leave almost at once. I am going to the other side of the Iron Curtain. I feel that that's where *you* should be going. I am really doing your work. Can you hear me clearly?"

"Quite clearly."

Perspiration had sprung out on Roscoe's forehead.

"If you Federal people would only go out for the real enemy, instead of wasting your time and energy pursuing a woman whose aims are identical with yours, the world might have a chance to recover itself. Don't you see that?"

"I hear what you say."

Sweetly musical laughter came over the line.

"Still thinking like a policeman! Are you really going to try to find me, Drake Roscoe? I am a small needle in the large haystack of Manhattan. And I shan't be here long. Don't worry about your English friend, McKeigh. I confess he was abducted. But he is deliriously happy with Viola. I have high hopes for the fruits of such a union. And now—may I make a few simple requests?"

"No harm done."

"Please see that my golden orfe in the pond are removed to a suitable aquarium. They are prize specimens. And don't let anyone destroy Satan, the barracuda. Have him shipped to Florida and let him go free. Then, I beg you, don't make yourself a nuisance to the League. Few of those worthy women even suspect my existence."

Sumuru was silent for a moment, until:

"May I ask you to tell Officer Rooney, who lent me a dollar towards Mrs. Murphy's taxi-fare, that he will be receiving a small present very shortly. Last of all—am I boring you? Mrs. Murphy should call on the law firm of Savile, Jones & Williamson. A charitable friend has left her an annuity. *Au revoir....*"

DA JUL 7 2014

CPSIA information can be obtained at www.ICGtesting.com
Printed in the USA
BVOW02s0513050314

346724BV00003B/574/P

9 781596 544482